TOMÁS
TAKES
CHARGE

· YOUNG AMERICA BOOK CLUB ·
EDUCATION CENTER · COLUMBUS, OHIO 43216

YOUNG AMERICA BOOK CLUB

presents

TOMÁS
TAKES
CHARGE

by CHARLENE JOY TALBOT

Illustrated by Reisie Lonette

LOTHROP, LEE & SHEPARD CO., INC.

NEW YORK

To Miss Carmie Wolfe,
who encouraged me in high school

*Four lines from PEGGY O'NEIL
by Harry Pease, Ed. G. Nelson and
Gilbert Dodge
Copyright 1921/Copyright Renewal 1949,
Leo Feist Inc., New York, N.Y.
Used by permission.*

YOUNG AMERICA BOOK CLUB EDITION

CONTENTS

1

MRS. MALLOY TAKES A STAND

Tomás Lorca stood in the open end of a wooden packing crate. He closed his eyes. I will count to twenty-five, he told himself. When I look, Papa will be coming. With a bag of food. No, two bags, one in each arm.

He counted, then looked. One way and the other. Except for a truck in the next block, the street was empty. Friday-night empty. From Friday night until Sunday evening, the bare loading docks along Greenwich Street, the huge locked doors, the vacant windows of the warehouses belonged to Tomás—Tomás and the twenty or so other people who lived in Washington Market.

The rest of the week, day and night, the trucks were there. They rumbled over the cobblestones, waited patiently in line until they could move ahead or back up across the sidewalks to the loading docks of the warehouse.

Tomás leaned against the rough, new-smelling boards of the crate and closed his eyes again. This time he would count to fifty. His thick hair was dusty black; his face, pale, except for the brown-purple shadows under his closed eyes. The shadows were from hunger, a hunger which had been growing for days until now he was seeing the barbecued chicken again, sizzling and browning inside a glass case. These days he always saw it inside the glass case.

Tomás was eleven and beginning to grow. The old red-striped T-shirt was too short. So were last year's suit pants, but his rubber-thong sandals, found in a trash can, fitted just right.

A summer evening breeze wandered up Greenwich Street from the Battery. It brought the smell of salt water. Even the smells changed on Friday night; no more whiffs of cinnamon or of roasting coffee until Monday morning.

He opened his eyes again at the count of fifty. A Market worker went shuffling around the corner of the building where the coffee was roasted. Nobody else.

Tomás climbed to the top of his crate and watched old Mrs. Stefano come out from the hot apartment house. She lived on the fifth floor. He watched her cross the street and sit on a loading dock.

A cruising patrol car passed, and then the Market watchman, driving his blue car.

The evening was cool for the first of July—in fact perfect. Soon the street lights came on. Tomás jumped to the sidewalk, gave the crate a farewell pat, and picked up the onion and two pimientos he had found. They had been lying inside the crate, like a present. It was past suppertime.

He stopped in the doorway of his building to take a last look at the quiet street. Although this was the island of Manhattan, where millions of people lived, most of the buildings in this small section were wholesale warehouses. The men who sold the fruit and vegetables, cheese and eggs, used only the ground floors of their buildings. They closed off the upper stories, leaving them empty.

One block away, and just as quiet on a Friday night, was the center of the Market—on Washington Street, the street for which the Market was named.

The apartment where Tomás lived was in one of the few apartment buildings left in the Market. Tomás climbed the three flights of stairs, pushed open the door, and stepped into the kitchen. His sister Fernanda looked up. Without asking, he knew what she wanted to know. He shook his head, No, Papa had not come.

Fernanda sat at the kitchen table where she had been leafing through one of her scrapbooks. The scrapbooks were her greatest treasures and she never tired of looking at the colored pictures she had pasted in them. Some were of rooms, with beautiful furniture. Other pages were filled with pictures of flowers, clothes and food. All the pictures had been cut from the magazines that Tomás brought her from time to time.

Whenever Fernanda was unhappy or upset, she opened one of her scrapbooks and imagined herself living in one of the beautiful rooms. She did this quite often.

She was paler than Tomás, and though she was fourteen, her big dark eyes had the wide look of a six year old. The blue nylon dress she wore was too small for her. Papa had bought it as a present long ago, hoping she would wear it when she went walking with him on Sundays. But she had not gone walking with him on Sundays. She would not.

Tomás put the onion and the pimientos on the table.

"Ay, Tomás!" Fernanda whispered.

"What is it? What's wrong?" he asked in Spanish.

"The Super," Fernanda said. "She has been here again."

Tomás dropped into one of the chairs at the table. "What did she say?"

"She said, 'Where is your father? I have not seen him in days.' "

"You didn't tell her!" Tomás held his breath.

"No! I said, 'Papa is working both day and night. That is why you have not seen him.' "

Tomás studied one of the magazine pictures upside down. "You told her right," he said.

"The rent is two weeks due," Fernanda continued. "She says she can wait no longer. She must tell the landlord."

Tomás gave this his full attention. "Papa will come home tonight. Or tomorrow."

"If not," Fernanda said, "I do not know what we will eat. We have only this onion, these pimientos, and a little flour."

"No more rice?"

Fernanda shook her head.

Tomás turned one ear to the door. Someone was mounting the stairs with a slow shuffle. It was the step of Mrs. Malloy, the Superintendent. She swept and mopped the halls and stairs, put out the garbage cans, and once a month collected the rent. Mrs. Malloy had a red, kindly face, a loud kindly voice, and a cat named Clancy.

They heard Mrs. Malloy pause, then sigh with relief as she reached the landing and shuffled along two steps . . . three, four . . . she was going past! No, she was stopping. Breathing heavily, she knocked on their door.

Fernanda looked at Tomás to see whether they were going to answer. Tomás nodded his head, yes. Fernanda opened the door.

Mrs. Malloy shuffled into the kitchen and without greeting either Tomás or Fernanda began talking. "Well, and I took it on myself to call the place where your papa works. I don't like the sound of it, I don't."

She looked in a worried way at the children and eased herself onto the third chair at the kitchen table.

11

"I telephoned the place where your papa works," she said again. "He ain't there any more. They told me he ain't there."

"He has a better job!" Tomás said.

Mrs. Malloy raised her shoulders in such a way that her head half disappeared between her great shoulders, like a turtle's.

"Then I'd like to know what's keeping him from paying the rent?" she asked. "Is he maybe saving up until he has money enough to buy the building?"

"He's too busy!" Tomás shouted. "He's so busy he forgets."

Mrs. Malloy looked at the bare shelves in the kitchen cupboard. She waved a hand at them. "That's for sure! And are you trying to tell me it's the same way he forgets to buy food?"

Tomás had no answer.

Mrs. Malloy shook a forefinger at them. "They haven't seen hide nor hair of him on the job for the last three weeks. Nor have the neighbors. And neither, my lambs, have you." Her voice turned soft. "The Lord love you, both of you, you'll have to face it. Tomás, Fernanda, your papa will not be coming back. Not right away, anyhow. Not soon enough to put any hot food inside the pair of you tonight."

Still Tomás said nothing.

"Mind, I don't say he won't *ever* come back. Only that for the time bein' we've got to find somebody to look after the two of you."

She paused again to catch her breath. The children watched her, wondering what she would say next.

She threw up her hands. "Sure now, you've a nice auntie or an uncle or even a cousin who'd be glad to have you over for a little visit?"

Tomás started to shake his head, but Mrs. Malloy went on.

"Well, then . . . I guess we'll just have to call Welfare on Monday. They take very good care of children at the Shelter, and they'll turn the city upside down to try to find your papa."

Tomás was thinking fast. "Oh, we won't need *Welfare*, Mrs. Malloy. We have a godmother in Brooklyn. She has already asked us to come there," he said without hesitation. "We will go on Sunday."

Mrs. Malloy leaned on the table and pushed herself to her feet. "And why didn't you tell me that right off? And save me all that worryin'?"

Her glance wandered around the kitchen. The gas range and the noisy refrigerator belonged to the landlord. Six plates, three cups, some glasses, bowls, and a few pans sat on the two shelves. The red and chrome table and four chairs were the only furniture in the room. She looked again at the empty cupboard.

"It'll take two shakes of a lamb's tail to heat up some fish cakes. There are plenty left from supper. I'll have Malloy bring them up to you." She turned to leave, then thought of something else. "And don't be worryin' over your furniture. Malloy'll cover it up and store it in the basement where nobody can get at it." She patted Fernanda's shoulder. "It'll be waitin' for you as soon as you come back from Brooklyn."

She opened the door. "And don't you set foot out of this place without givin' me your godmother's name and address. Hear?"

14

They heard her shuffle down the stairs. When she was out of earshot, Fernanda whispered to Tomás.

"Why did you tell her that, about the godmother?"

He waited to answer until he heard Mrs. Malloy's door slam.

"Because I had to. You don't want to go to Welfare, do you?"

"No," Fernanda answered in Spanish. "I do not want to go anywhere. But I know we cannot stay here. The police will throw us out as they did the Garcías. Tomás," she said, looking hard at her brother, "in the street I shall die." She was about to cry.

"We won't be thrown in the street," Tomás assured her, though he felt far from sure.

He, too, was thinking of the Garcías. Juan García's father had also gone away and not come back. From the window Tomás and Fernanda had watched the Garcías' furniture being put on the street. Then the Welfare came and took the Garcías away. People said Welfare was good, but all Tomás knew for sure was that he never saw Juan García again.

For himself he was not so much afraid as for Fernanda. She was like Clancy, Mrs. Malloy's cat. Clancy was seven. He had been born in Mrs. Malloy's apartment and had never been out of it. Mrs. Malloy said he was an apartment cat.

Fernanda was an apartment girl. She had been born in Puerto Rico. When she was two years old, Papa and

Mama and Grandmama had brought her to New York with them. But she didn't remember that. She only knew this apartment on the fifth floor. Papa and Mama worked all day. Grandmama could not climb up and down so many stairs, so she never took Fernanda outdoors.

Soon after Tomás was born, Mama died.

Grandmama took care of Tomás and Fernanda. But she did not send Fernanda to school, because she did not think girls needed to learn to read and write. Fernanda was glad. She was afraid of going out of the house, and the thought of walking through the open streets terrified her. She wanted to stay inside, to be under a roof all the time. She had seen the huge trucks and heard them snorting, honking, hissing, and braking as they roared forward or backed up.

Tomás was different. As soon as he could walk, he had unlatched the door of the apartment, explored the hall, and fallen down a flight of stairs. As soon as he could climb downstairs without falling, he ran away. A neighbor brought him back, but he ran away almost every day after that—and came back every night. When summer came, he played on the streets with the older children from the tenement in the next block, and from them he learned how to dodge cars and trucks.

When he was five, his father said he would have to go to school. He went with two second graders—Juan

García and Raimundo Sánchez who were looked after and bossed by Loretta, Juan's older sister. Mornings, they waited together for the school bus.

Then Grandmama died. That was terrible. Luckily Fernanda had learned how to sew and cook and clean the house. As fast as Tomás learned himself, he taught Fernanda how to speak and to read English. And Papa worked hard to keep his family together. But now Papa was lost.

"Where are we going?" Fernanda asked. "Tomás, what are we going to do?"

"I don't know." He got up from the chair and wandered to the window. The view was a wall, twenty feet away. Its old bricks had turned orange, pink, rich brown and blue. The windows in the wall had iron shutters. One pair unfastened easily. They whined and banged when the wind blew.

Tomás snapped his fingers. "I have an idea. I will tell you in the morning what my idea is."

2

TOMÁS TAKES CHARGE

Tomás woke early and remembered the leftover fish cakes. They had saved two each for breakfast. He jumped out of bed, but instead of running to the kitchen to get them, he ran to look at Papa's bed. The blue bedspread was smooth. The bed was empty.

He went to the kitchen, put water on to boil for the coffee, and then dressed.

While he ate his fish cakes, he thought about his plan. As soon as he finished eating, he told Fernanda he was going out but that he would be back very soon.

Two blocks down Greenwich Street was the apartment house were Raimundo Sánchez had lived. It, too, was sandwiched between warehouses. No children of school age lived in the building now, but Tomás knew that the Pérez and Salvador families lived on the top floor. Their children were babies. Bert, the taxi driver, lived on the third floor.

Tomás ran all the way to this building and climbed up four flights of stairs. There was a shorter flight to

the roof. He made it without meeting anyone.

Unhooking the door, he stepped out onto the flat, tarred roof. The steamy air smelled of tar and the ocean. On one side he looked up at the higher roof of the next building. On the other, a low wall separated the roof he stood on from the roof of the adjoining building. Tomás walked on tiptoe to this wall, stepped on it, and jumped down on the roof below.

Downtown he could see the skyscrapers in the haze. To the west and very close, the Hudson River sparkled where the sun hit it. He looked at the back of a great

neon sign on a roof not far away. At night it changed from a lemon to an orange, blinking back and forth.

The river was deep here, and wide, already part of the ocean. On the other side of it, under the giant clock, was New Jersey. River traffic had stopped for the weekend. The tugboats had docked, their crews gone home. A white Belgian ship tied to a pier two blocks away looked near enough for Tomás to be able to jump on its deck.

Tomás knew all about the building whose roof he was standing on, because once he and Juan and Raimundo had explored all the buildings in the neighborhood. Only the ground floor of this building was used. Above the ground floor the stairway was boarded over; so was the roof door leading down into the building. All the windows which faced the street were covered with tin. The broken panes of the back windows let in light, air, and pigeons. It would be a perfect place for him and Fernanda to live—and nobody would think of looking for them here.

Tomás headed for the fire escape, the old-fashioned iron-ladder kind, at the back of the building. He climbed down it from the roof and entered the top floor of the building through a broken window. Once inside he made his way to the big front room. A little light crept in through the cracks around the sealed windows. As his eyes grew used to the dim light, he saw a soot-blackened fireplace on the inside wall. Good! They could build a fire, and Fernanda could cook over it, like the Pilgrims.

The floor was thick with soot and grime. A mattress lay opposite the fireplace. It was in pretty good shape, but also covered with soot. Fernanda could clean the floor and the mattress and she could sleep in this room.

Among some junk and broken plaster in one of the other rooms was a pad from a baby's crib. He would have to use that. Also he would clean up that room, and it would be his.

22

You could lock the door to the front room from the inside. Lucky! If anybody came, he and Fernanda could lock themselves in. He nodded. They would hide here till Papa came home. It might even be fun, like living in a secret tower.

He walked back to the fire-escape window, kicking small chunks of fallen plaster out of his way. The floor was dirty, and glass lay splintered under the three back windows. But light streamed in. From where Tomás stood he could see a wide stretch of sky, a row of tarred roofs, and leaning chimneys.

Most of the windows of the buildings in the back had dirty or missing panes, which meant those floors were empty. One row was tight-shuttered. No one would be able to look in on them.

This will please Fernanda, he thought as he climbed the ladder. She can even have sun and air, without going out to the street, and no people to frighten her.

When he walked into his own kitchen a few minutes later, Fernanda was sitting at the red-topped table, waiting.

He described the place he had found. "We will hide there," he explained. "Papa will surely come in a day or two."

Fernanda wanted to know how Papa would find them.

"How will he find us if Welfare takes us?" Tomás asked. "This way, someone will see me in the street, and they will say, 'Your Papa is looking for you.' Then we will go home."

"I think you are crazy!" Fernanda thrust out her lip and sat looking stubborn.

"Do you want to go to Welfare then?" Tomás asked. "They'll *make* you go to school. To first grade, with little kids. They'll make you *go outside,* too. All the time."

Fernanda's outthrust lower lip went slowly back where it belonged. "Maybe you're not so crazy," she said.

"Just wait!" Tomás said. "You'll like it, you'll see! I bet even Papa will like it so much he'll want to live there with us."

Fernanda closed her scrapbook and leaned back. She gave him a serious look. "Very well, Tomás. We will do as you say."

Tomás slapped the table. "Good! Let's see what we have to take." He jumped up and started for the bedroom.

"Wait!" Fernanda called. "What are we going to eat?"

He came back and perched on the edge of his chair. "Peppers and onions. I found two, I can find more. Other things fall off the trucks and out of baskets. I've seen them. Things Americans eat." He made a face. "Carrots and potatoes and green leaves. If they eat them, we can."

Fernanda clapped her hand to her mouth. "Tomás—the godmother in Brooklyn! You told Mrs. Malloy."

"Ah, yes." Tomás scratched his head. Suddenly he nodded. "The telephone book. In a telephone booth in a drug store I have seen a whole book for Brooklyn. I will go and pick out a godmother for Mrs. Malloy."

Fernanda giggled, then shrugged her shoulders.

Tomás jumped up again and went to the cupboard. "We must think what we want to take. Plates." He took two from the shelf. "Two cups, two glasses—" He began bringing the dishes to the table. "It is like moving. We are going to live in a new house."

Fernanda joined the game. She opened two brown paper shopping bags and stood them on the floor. Into one, she put her red dress and her yellow dress, neatly folded, and her most prized article of clothing, her pink quilted nylon robe, a present from Mrs. Malloy. Into the other, she put Tomás's four shirts and three T-shirts, his blue pullover sweater, his other pair of undershorts. She left his winter coat hanging in the closet.

Tomás folded their red blankets, laid two pillows on top and rolled them into a bundle which he tied with rope. He put the bundle on his head. "I'll take these now," he said from under the bundle. "We will have to sleep here tonight—because we told Mrs. Malloy we would leave tomorrow. We'll use the bedding from Papa's bed."

He took the bundles to the vacant building.

In the afternoon he made another trip, carrying a plastic bucket filled with their dishes, glasses, saucepan and frying pan. In the other hand he carried a broom. So far he had met no one to question him or wonder what he was doing. But now, as he was going down the stairs from the roof for the last time, he heard the heavy tread of a man coming up.

Tomás stopped on one foot in the middle of the fourth floor hall. Should he turn around, sneak back up? He leaned over the bannister and peered down. He could see the shine of a metal badge on the man's cap. Then the man moved into the light from the dim bulb in the ceiling of the hall below, and Tomás saw the black crown of a cap and the shoulder of a faded plaid shirt. It was Bert, the taxi driver.

Tomás waited until the door on the third floor closed. The tenants of this building must not see him. Not when he could help it.

When he got back home, he found Mrs. Malloy had sent up some stew. Fernanda turned on the TV while they ate. When they finished and Fernanda had washed the dishes, they lay across Papa's unused bed and watched one program after another until very late. They did not think about Papa's being gone or even about having to hide until he came back.

3

CAVE DWELLERS

The faint, rich tones of the City Hall clock striking ten wakened Tomás on Sunday morning. The sun was streaming between the flowery curtains. He lay looking at the apartment. He imagined how it would look without furniture.

He got up. At the kitchen sink he washed his face and combed his hair. He brushed his teeth, left the toothpaste open for Fernanda, and put his toothbrush in the shopping bag with his clothes.

Fernanda yawned sleepily as she came into the kitchen. She boiled water, and they each drank a cup of black coffee for breakfast. Luckily the big jar of instant coffee was still half full.

"I wish we could take the TV," she said wistfully.

"Well, we can't," Tomás said firmly. "But I'll get you some more old magazines for your scrapbooks."

"My scrapbooks!" Fernanda put her hand over her mouth. "I was forgetting them!"

She ran to her room and returned with her nine

spiral-bound notebooks, her scissors, and a jar of paste. How *could* she have forgotten them! They held her secret life, and all her dreams.

At eleven o'clock when church-going tenants would be at Mass and the others might still be sleeping, Tomás made a trip to the hideout. He took what food remained—half a jar of pickles, a jar of mustard, salt, pepper, a nearly full bottle of oil, a sack of flour. And the precious coffee.

In front of the other building he met Bert.

"Hi, kid, how's tricks?" Bert asked as he walked by.

"Okay." Tomás smiled, and set the shopping bag on the sidewalk as though resting. He waited until Bert had turned the corner before he darted into the hallway.

On the top floor the door to one apartment stood open. Tomás heard voices, but he slipped past without being seen. He crossed the two rooftops, climbed down the fire-escape ladder to the landing and through the window into the back room of the hideout.

In the dark front room, he set the groceries down by the fireplace. He swept a layer of grit from the mattress that Fernanda would sleep on and tried to sweep the room. But he raised such a choking dust that he had to sit in the open back window to wait for it to settle. A pigeon walked babbling along the parapet of the opposite roof. It saw Tomás, paused, and watched him without interest.

Tomás went back into the front room and again

swept up such a dust storm that it almost choked him and he had to leave the hideout. He ran across the roofs and down the stairs. Either the Pérez or the Salvador family—he couldn't tell which—went downstairs ahead of him. He waited a few minutes before going out to the street. Then he raced around the corner.

"Once we're moved in, I won't go out so often," he said to himself. "And when I'm out, I'll stay out. Or maybe I'll only go out late at night after everybody's asleep."

Instead of going straight back to Fernanda, he toured the telephone booths. Sometimes in the coin-return slots he found forgotten dimes.

It was one o'clock when he went into the Chambers Street luncheonette, found a Brooklyn telephone book, and leafed through it. In the R's he found *Mrs. Fernanda Ravello.* Perfect! She could be the godmother Fernanda was named for.

He asked the counterman politely to lend him a pencil. He copied the name and address on a scrap of paper. He deliberately did *not* copy the phone number.

He tucked the paper into his pocket and returned the pencil. He then went on up the street and strolled into every open luncheonette, drug store, and bar. He slid two fingers into the black coin-return cup in every unoccupied telephone booth, was lucky or unlucky, and strolled out again.

Once, a long time ago, he had pressed the coin-return and two quarters, three dimes and a nickel had slipped smoothly into his hand. Today his luck was nothing like that. Only two dimes. But when he added the nickel he had collected for returning a soda bottle left on a loading dock, the total was twenty-five cents.

It was time to go home. As he circled back, he thought how he would spend the money: fifteen cents would buy a pound of beans or a pound of rice, whichever Fernanda wanted. He would let her decide. That left ten cents. With another nickel he could buy half a dozen cracked eggs from the egg wholesaler tomorrow.

Tomás liked arithmetic—even decimals and fractions. He found it useful. He liked knowing that if 15 cents would buy six eggs, 10 cents would buy four. If the wholesale man did not know, Tomás would tell him.

He went up to the apartment and showed Fernanda the day's profit and the name of the godmother.

"She must be a nice lady," Fernanda said.

"Why?"

"She has a nice name."

Tomás smiled and looked up from stacking the two dimes and the nickel.

"Anything to eat?"

"Peppers and onion," Fernanda said. While Tomás was out she had sliced them into a pan with water and put it on the stove to stew. She had found one dried-up frankfurter at the back of the refrigerator, sliced that, and put it in, too. In the water the frankfurter grew fat again.

"That was pretty good," Tomás said when they were drinking their coffee. He walked over to the open window.

The street, quiet since Friday evening, was beginning to grow lively. A long silver refrigerator truck pulled up in front of their building. The driver disappeared but he left the cooling unit whirring on its shelf above the cab of the truck. A red truck parked across the street, and a green one parked in front of it.

Tomás turned on the television. He lay on his stomach across the bed, watching a cowboy movie.

"When are we going?" Fernanda asked.

"About nine o'clock," Tomás said. "By that time it will be dark and no one will see us." He got up and rummaged in a drawer.

By six o'clock, the Market was in full swing—trucks honking, motors idling, and the familiar shouts of men guiding drivers into parking spaces or up to the loading docks.

"C'mon back, c'mon back, c'mon back. . . . Hold it. . . . HOLD IT!"

At six-thirty, when the movie ended, Tomás's stomach felt as though it had never had anything in it. But there was no more food.

"What if I go down and get a bag of potato chips?" he asked. "Tomorrow I will find money for rice."

Fernanda's eyes brightened. She loved potato chips.

The ten-cent bags at the luncheonette looked smaller than ever. He bought two. I'll save one to eat in our new place, he decided.

On the way back, he passed the open doors of the place which packaged vegetables for supermarkets and grocery stores. Spinach, kale, carrots, and cabbage arrived in baskets and crates and left in small bulging bags.

On the loading dock, huge bins on casters stood filled with cabbage leaves, celery tops, and spinach. Tomás had often seen broken carrots in them, and small leafy stalks of celery, but he had never thought of them as food. He remembered how surprised he had been to hear his teacher say once that raw carrots, celery, and other vegetables were good for children. Tomás wondered. But he was hungrier than usual and though he preferred fried bananas the way Fernanda cooked them, he would try some of this raw stuff.

With the bags of potato chips in one hand, he picked up a carrot with the other and smelled it. He remembered telling Fernanda about how he would eat vegetables. He took a bite. It tasted like raw potato. He bit into a stalk of celery. He shrugged. It did not taste like food. He could understand why this place threw so much of it away. But since it was free and good for you, he would take some.

When Papa came home, they would eat pork the

first night, and chicken the second, with plenty of good, filling rice.

He went back upstairs and suggested to Fernanda that she eat a stalk of celery. She shook her head, making her hair fly back and forth.

"Here. Eat potato chips then," Tomás said quickly.

She ran to the front room and put her head under the bedclothes. Tomás followed.

"Come on," he coaxed. "I bought them for you. Me. I like this."

He chomped on a carrot. The chewing was so loud that Fernanda heard it even under the bedclothes. She giggled. She sat up, pushing back her dark hair. "Bugs Bunny!" Fernanda laughed. "You sound like Bugs Bunny."

By nine o'clock lights were coming on outside— yellow street lights, white headlights, red tail lights.

"We'd better start," Tomás said.

His legs felt stiff with excitement. He and Fernanda each took a shopping bag and shut the door of their apartment behind them. Fernanda paused. Tomás was afraid she would turn back, but she followed him down the stairs to Mrs. Malloy's.

They could hear the television, and it was a minute after they knocked before Mrs. Malloy opened the door. Mr. Malloy was sitting with his shoes off. His arms were huge and round; his fist curved, holding a glass.

"So late!" Mrs. Malloy cried.

Tomás shrugged. "Fernanda won't be so scared after dark."

He held out the paper with the godmother's name and address on it. Mrs. Malloy reached out and took it as she said, "Come in! Come in! You can't just hand me your new address, say goodbye, and leave. Only the good Lord knows when we'll see you again! What would you say to a dish of ice cream before you take off?"

Tomás hesitated. He was afraid of what Fernanda might do. She often visited Mrs. Malloy. Now she might refuse to leave.

But Fernanda was leaning her shopping bag against the wall. Tomás did the same and followed her into the room.

Mr. Malloy motioned them to chairs as he said, "Now don't be eating your hearts out. Lorca will show up in a day or two." He meant Papa.

"Sure he will. Sure as you're sittin' here he will. But this ice cream's gonna melt before then, so I'd advise you to eat it now," Mrs. Malloy said.

She had brought two boxes from the refrigerator— chocolate ice cream and vanilla. She scooped big spoonfuls into red plastic bowls. Fernanda got more vanilla; Tomás, more chocolate. They sat at Mrs. Malloy's plastic-covered table to eat it.

Almost everything in Mrs. Malloy's house was plastic. Red roses on the table made every meal like a party. Between the plastic curtains, red plastic geraniums on the window sills never withered, never stopped blooming. Plastic lace doilies on the television and on the end tables made white curlicues against the dark wood. Green plastic ivy curled around the blue television lamp.

Tomás touched the harmless thorns of the roses in their plastic basket.

Clancy rubbed against Tomás's leg and purred, wanting to lick the bowl.

"Clancy," Tomás said, "you're too fat."

Tomás scraped the bowl, licked the spoon, and sat back, swinging his legs. Ice cream certainly tasted better than carrots.

He wished he wasn't so worried.

"Come," he said to Fernanda, "we better go."

Mrs. Malloy put the paper with the godmother's name and address into a drawer.

"Now, don't worry. Either of you," she said. "I'll phone you or your papa will, soon as he comes home. You'll just be gone long enough for a nice little visit."

Tomás nodded. Mrs. Malloy patted his head and kissed Fernanda's cheek. Fernanda's sad, frightened eyes filled with tears.

"Don't worry. There's nothing to worry about. Honest," Mrs. Malloy told her. "You kids are gonna have a wonderful time in Brooklyn."

"And don't get on the wrong subway," said Mr. Malloy, turning his head from the television for the first time.

Mrs. Malloy watched them down the steps. Tomás called goodbye. When they were out of sight, they heard the door close. Fernanda hesitated.

"Come on," he said, and took her hand.

Fernanda behaved all right until Tomás opened the street door. Then she put her back against the wall.

"No!" she cried.

Tomás shushed her. He was afraid she would bolt back upstairs the way Clancy did.

"Come on," he whispered fiercely. "You cannot go back now. Mrs. Malloy will find out we told a lie. She will call Welfare."

"I am afraid," Fernanda whimpered.

"You must come. You have to," Tomás said, "even if you are afraid. Terrible things will happen to us if you do not."

He dug in his shopping bag and pulled out his sweater. He put it over her head, like a kerchief, tying the sleeves loosely under her chin. "Come on. That's a magic sweater. With than on, nobody can see you. Shut your eyes."

He opened the door and pushed her ahead of him onto the sidewalk. The door banged shut.

Hand in hand, each carrying a shopping bag, they started down the street.

"Just a little further," he said soothingly. "Just one more block."

She held his fingers in so tight a grip that they hurt, but he dared not say so.

At last they reached the other building. They had gone up one flight when they heard people coming in below. Fernanda went up the steps like a frightened cat.

At the door to the roof Tomás whispered, "Open it."

She stepped out on the roof. "No!" she gasped, and turned back. Tomás blocked the way.

"Go on!" he said in a whisper. He shoved her out and closed the door behind him.

Fernanda shrank against the door frame. Tomás understood a little of how she must feel. Up here, out of the shadowy canyons of warehouses and buildings, the sky was still light. It spread overhead, roofless, surrounding them in every direction.

"Come on," he urged.

Fernanda whimpered, pressing tighter against the wall. Tomás opened the door a crack. In the hall below was the Salvador family. Mr. Salvador was turning the key in their lock.

Tomás shut the door again and waved Fernanda toward the other roof.

"Come on. Before those people hear us."

He took her hand and pulled. Once away from the wall, she moved willingly enough, though he could feel her terror in her stiff fingers.

"Just a little further," he coaxed. "We're almost there."

When they reached the fire-escape ladder, he took her shopping bag.

"Climb down to the iron landing," he whispered to her. "Wait for me there."

Tomás put the two shopping bags near the edge of the roof where he could reach them, climbed partway down the ladder and picked up the bags again.

"Here," he said, handing them down to Fernanda. "Take them. Let go the railing! You can't fall."

She did as he told her, but she gasped and clutched the railing as he landed beside her with a jump that shook the iron slats of the landing.

"All right, all right," he said. "Go on in. I'm right behind you. As soon as we get inside I'll light a candle."

She crouched on the window sill, reached one foot tentatively down to the floor, said, "Ah," as she felt it, and stepped inside.

Tomás crawled in after her. He stood shifting his feet uncomfortably on the rubble-covered floor while he hunted for matches and a candle.

"Is this it?" she whispered.

"Yes. It's dark in here now, but in the morning you'll see how nice it is. Now we go up front."

In the front room she stood peering around.

"Put your bag down," he said. He ran over and shot the bolt on the door. "See, even a lock." He spread his arms. "Nice, eh? You like it, don't you? *Don't* you, Fernanda?"

Fernanda put her shopping bag on the floor, leaning it against her leg. "I don't know." But she was beginning to feel safe again. The brown walls and dirty floor made the room seem like a cave.

Tomás knelt by the fireplace and struck a match. The paper he had thrown into it while cleaning, caught fire and gave off an orange glow.

Fernanda's great dark eyes reflected the fire. Light fell on her smooth pale cheeks and forehead, on the black hair framing her face. Tomás remembered a picture of people dressed in skins standing around a fire.

"You look just like a cave dweller," he cried. He sat back on the floor, hugging his knees. "We're both cave dwellers."

Fernanda crouched in front of the fire beside him. "Well?" he demanded. "Do you like it?"

"Yes." Now she was smiling faintly. She rubbed one finger along a floor board. "It is *very* dirty." Tomás knew she was thinking pleasurably of sweeping it.

She looked around. "Is there something to sit on?"

"Sit on this." He dragged forward the mattress on which he had spread some bedding. "Tomorrow I'll get some boxes to sit on and to put things in."

He fished in his shopping bag and took out the second sack of potato chips. *"Mira."* He handed them to Fernanda. "Look, a surprise!"

Fernanda laughed and smoothed back her hair. Her teeth glinted as she bit the cellophane and tore open the bag. "What a day! Potato chips and ice cream both. But I am sorry we lied to Mrs. Malloy."

Tomás nodded. "Me, too. But when Papa comes back next week, she'll be glad she didn't give us to Welfare."

"Is this room always so dark?"

"Just about," Tomás said. "This will be your sleeping cave. I will sleep in the next room. It gets light out that way." He nodded toward the back.

"Where will I cook?" she asked.

"In the fireplace."

Fernanda looked at him. "How?"

"*How?*" Tomás shouted. "The way the Cave women did, and pioneers and Puritans. Everybody used to. If you'd go to school, you wouldn't be so dumb."

Fernanda got up without saying anything and went to her bed. The fire had died down, and the room grew black again.

Tomás stood up. "Do you want the candle?" Fernanda did not answer so he took it with him into the room that was to be his.

He blew out the candle and lay down on his hard mattress feeling pleased. The things they needed were here; Fernanda was here. They were safe. All they had to do now was keep hidden till Papa came back.

The noises of the Market sounded far away. Then something scuttled inside the wall. He listened. A small animal ran across the roof. The scrabbling in the wall changed to gnawing.

"What's that?" Fernanda called out in alarm.

"Must be rats," he called back. "Don't be afraid. Tomorrow I'll get a cat."

Reassured, Fernanda lay down again, and in a little while they were both asleep.

4

FOOD, FIRE, WATER

The next morning in the gray light that leaked in from around the windows, it took Tomás a few seconds to remember where he was. He turned over.

Fernanda was already awake and called out to him, "Where's the bathroom?"

"Out there. The bathroom is in the hall."

She got up, put on her dress, and unlocked the door. He heard plaster crunching under her feet as she walked down the hall. But in a minute she was back.

"Tomás—" She stopped in the doorway. "Tomás, there's no water! None in the sink or in the bathroom."

Tomás jumped up. "Water! I never thought of it."

He started for the kitchen. Fernanda followed.

"We can not wash or make coffee! What are we going to do?" she demanded. "How can we live here?"

Tomás turned on the faucets in the sink. No water. Under the sink he ran his hand down the pipe until it touched a small, round wheel which he began to turn. It turned easily. Fernanda stopped talking. She watched the sink, but no water spurted from the faucets.

"Ay," she sighed. "I wish it was true that we did have a godmother in Brooklyn."

"You don't even know where Brooklyn is," Tomás reminded her crossly.

She clasped her hands and looked out at the early-morning sky. "But it is nice here," she said.

Tomás stood thinking. One time last winter in the other building there had been trouble with the water. He had followed the plumber from floor to floor. He remembered there had been a valve on a lower floor which turned all the water off and on at once. If this building had such a valve, perhaps he could turn the water on now.

He made his way down the dark, dirty stairs, flight by flight. He searched for the valve on each floor. I should have thought of water, he scolded himself. This camping is not easy.

He found the valve he was looking for on the lowest of the closed-off floors, in the kitchen beside the sink. But when he tried to turn it, it refused to budge.

Very well, he could take care of that. Again he went from floor to floor until he found a scrap of wire and two small boards. The boards were about a foot long and an inch thick. He fastened them loosely together with the wire. Raimundo had taught him last summer how to use such a homemade wrench to unscrew the big bolt on the fire hydrant so they could play in the water.

He took his wrench back downstairs again and forced the valve to turn. A sound of rattling in the pipes rewarded him. Water was beginning to flow.

"Whew!" he said, sitting back and listening to the chug, pop, and bang as the water forced air out of the pipes.

Upstairs he found Fernanda watching brown water spurt from the choking sink faucets. In the bathroom he heard the tank filling.

He brought more scraps of wood up from the floor below where he also found some bricks and an old icebox grill. He carried these up and put two bricks in the fireplace. He set the grill on top of them and built a fire in between.

In the kitchen, the water was running clear. Fernanda was washing her hands and face at the sink. He saw she had braided her hair—a good sign.

"We forgot the soap," she exclaimed.

"I will buy some," Tomás said grandly. He filled a pan with water for coffee. "Your stove is ready. Come see."

When the water boiled, they made their coffee and went to sit in the back windows to drink it. Today the air, blowing fresh from the sea, made breathing a pleasure.

Tomás produced the nickel from his pocket and showed it to Fernanda. "Do you want soap—or rice? I have to find at least another nickel before I can get either one."

"Soap," she said.

"Oh, Fernanda, you always want everything so clean. I'm hungry."

"Then get rice," Fernanda said.

Crossing the roofs, Tomás realized it was very early, too early to buy rice. The big passenger liners were just coming up the river. When the first one was near enough for him to read the name on the bow he saw it was the *Constitution*. The *Leonardo* was close behind. He watched until a high building hid them from view. Then he went downstairs.

He would look around for boxes to use as furniture. A crisp pimiento lay in the middle of the street. Wondering how it had escaped the wheels of the trucks, he picked it up. Farther on, he found another. Then in the gutter, two sweet potatoes. He picked up an empty onion bag of purple mesh and put the vegetables in it.

At the corner he stared in delight. Here were riches: the street cleaners had made a big pile of broken crates, cartons, paper, cardboard, and discarded fruits and vegetables. He picked out a long green fruit which felt furry and a small yellow one which felt smooth and dusty.

"Finding anything, kid?"

Tomás jumped. It was the street cleaner. He showed him the yellow and green fruit. "What are these?" he asked.

"Squash," the street cleaner answered. "That's zucchini—" he pointed to the green one. "I don't know what the other one's called. It's good for you, though." He took off his glove and patted Tomás's thick hair. "Make your hair curl." He winked.

Tomás smiled back. "Does it have vitamins?"

"It's jumping with vitamins."

The street cleaner turned his back and began to

push his broom along the gutter. Then he stopped and looked back.

"There are some bananas down at the corner, if you want them." He pointed to the corner.

Tomás saw a pile of green and black banana stalks against a building.

"Thanks!" he shouted, running toward them, swinging the purple bag.

Sure enough, next to the stalks Tomás found two barrels full of green and yellow bananas and shredded paper. Every banana was damaged, its yellow skin bruised black or torn open, but parts looked good. Tomás peeled one, broke off the good part, and tasted it. His brown eyes widened. It *was* good! He could hardly believe they were being thrown out.

His mouth full of banana, his eyes sparkling, he looked like a chipmunk.

He dug down into each barrel as far as he could reach and filled the bag in no time at all. When he picked it up, it was heavy.

He had wanted to take up some wood for the fireplace, and two boxes to sit on. He also had to buy rice. There was no other way: he would have to make two trips.

On the way back, he found a clean crate and four Coke bottles. After putting the bag of bananas and vegetables into the crate, he promptly turned the Coke bottles into cash. Then, carrying the crate in both arms, he started upstairs.

His timing was wrong. As he set foot on the third floor, Bert's door opened. Bert came out, settling his taxi-driver hat on his head.

"Hiya, kid," Bert shouted.

Tomás backed against the wall for Bert to pass.

"You're getting to be quite a visitor," Bert said jovially.

Tomás gulped. At that instant a door slammed on the top floor. He heard the quick tap of high-heeled shoes on the stairs and saw the round brown calves and tiny feet of Mrs. Pérez.

"I'm baby-sitting for Mrs. Pérez," Tomás said. He spoke rapidly so Mrs. Pérez, who might speak English, would not understand.

"Good for you," Bert said. He poked the sack. "What you got there?"

"Bananas. For the baby. Want one?"

"Naw. Just had my coffee."

Mrs. Pérez reached the third floor landing. Bert turned and lifted his cap. "Morning, ma'am."

"Good morning," she answered.

Tomás spoke rapidly to her in Spanish. Bert caught the word '*bebé* sitter' as he plunged on downstairs.

Tomás was asking Mrs. Pérez if she needed a baby sitter.

She looked at him, surprised. "Not today," she said.

"Perhaps tomorrow?" Tomás suggested.

"*Sí,* tomorrow. Perhaps." She, too, hurried downstairs.

Tomás chuckled as he lugged the box and bananas on up to the roof. Now he had an excuse for being there. Perhaps Mrs. Pérez or Mrs. Salvador would let him baby sit. He would ask them every morning.

He was tiptoeing across the roof when white smoke began to pour out of the chimney above their hideout. He gasped. The watchman, the tenants from this building, anyone who happened to be looking, could see it.

As fast as he could he hurried down to Fernanda.

"What did you put on the fire?" he shouted.

"Some dirty old papers. Why?"

"It's smoking like crazy." He ran to the front room. He struck a match to the smoldering papers and flames leapt up, driving one large puff of smoke out into the room. "Like a smoke signal," he thought, "like a smoke signal to Welfare."

He went to the back room and knelt beside the window for a while, watching to see if anyone was going to come. Nothing happened. He sighed with relief and took the bananas out of the crate.

Fernanda was astonished to see so many.

They peeled one after another and ate and laughed until they were full. And still there were five bananas left. Tomás started to put them on the shelf above the sink.

"Wait," Fernanda cried. She wrung out a gray rag and wiped it across the shelf. The rag came away covered with black mud.

50

"Ugh!" she said, wrinkling her nose. "Everything here is so dirty."

"What if we wash the floor?" Tomás asked. "Then there will be no dust."

"We'll have mud!" Fernanda said. The job looked so hopeless she shrugged her shoulders and began to laugh. "If Mrs. Malloy could see us now." She giggled, throwing up her hands the way Mrs. Malloy did.

"We have water and a cooking place, and bananas," Tomás said gaily. "Now I'm going out to buy rice."

5

A COOKSTOVE

Monday passed, and Tuesday and Wednesday. Each morning Tomás found more fruit and vegetables than he and Fernanda could eat. Sometimes he found whole boxfuls stacked on the curb, waiting for the garbage trucks.

One morning he found a box of pears. Half were brown and mushy, but some were yellow—ripe and juicy, perfect for eating.

The first time he brought Fernanda two cucumbers he asked anxiously, "Can you cut off that soft part? Is the other part still good?"

"It looks good," she said. "Wait a moment."

She ran from the open-air back room through the hall to the cave room. Tomás stared after her frowning, trying to remember. No, he thought, slowly nodding his head, I have never seen her run before. She has always crept about with a shuffle like Grandmama.

She came flying back with one of the brown-covered spiral books and began leafing through the colored pages of pictures. She found the one she was hunting for and pointed at it. A great copper-colored pot filled the page. In it orange and green vegetables floated in a brown sauce.

"There," she said. "What does that say?"

Tomás smacked his lips. "Can you make that?"

"Maybe, if the butcher would give you a bone for broth. What does it say?"

"You read it," Tomás insisted.

As soon as he had begun to read in first grade, he had brought his books home to show Fernanda. In his pride at learning CAT and HEN and THE, he had taught her the words and awakened her interest in reading and spelling. She understood what she read, but she had trouble saying the English words aloud.

"Stew of spring vegetables," she read slowly, pronouncing with difficulty the list of things needed to make it. "Can you find some of these?" she asked.

Most of them he had never heard of, but he promised to try. "Anyway, it says here," he pointed out, "almost all vegetables go well in a stew."

The butcher gave him a nice meaty bone. He searched till he found carrots, an onion, a potato, some stalks of celery, and green peppers. The stew did not look as pretty as the one in the picture, but it tasted good. Fernanda was terribly proud.

"It's good like Mrs. Malloy's," she said.

"Better!" Tomás declared.

He had never been so busy. He quickly learned the habits of everyone in the building. Whenever he chanced to meet Mrs. Pérez or Mrs. Salvador, he asked if they wanted a baby sitter. On Wednesday, Mrs. Pérez said yes. He stayed with three-year-old Fidel while she went shopping.

She paid him enough to buy soap and bread and candy.

On Thursday he spent the afternoon watching both little Fidel and the Salvador baby while their mothers went to a movie. Both women thought he still lived in Mrs. Malloy's building.

With that day's money in his pocket, he walked to Canal Street. He bought candles. At the secondhand bookstore he bought Fernanda an old magazine. He had money left over! He jingled it in his pocket and walked home whistling.

He felt very pleased with himself. He could do as well as Papa at providing for them. Except a television set. We have not been hungry all week' though, he thought. Before, we were often hungry.

They had been careful not to light fires until after dark when the smoke could not be seen. They missed their hot morning coffee, but Tomás solved that problem, too.

Several blocks down the street stood the warehouse of a company which collected waste paper. When their trucks brought other trash, it was piled overnight on the sidewalk. Tomás began to visit the place every evening.

He found a little office chair with four wheels, the leather seat only a little torn. He took it home. The following evening under piles of wooden packing boxes and neon tubes, he found a cup and two pie tins. On Friday night he made his best find—a small kerosene stove with two burners, and yards and yards of yellow cloth.

He was so excited he couldn't think. How could he carry the stove and the cloth? How could he carry even the stove to the hideout? Yet how could he leave the yellow cloth behind? He danced about looking for something to haul the stove on, wishing he had a wire shopping cart with wheels.

He spotted an end of clothesline rope and pulled at it. It turned out to be long enough to tie around the stove. Could he then hoist it on his shoulders, the way he'd seen movers do?

He was wrapping it around the stove when a worker from the Market came along. He didn't seem to be in a hurry. Tomás felt in his pocket. A dime and a quarter. He looked back and forth from the stove to the cloth and made up his mind.

He stepped in front of the man.

"Hey, mister," he said, "could you help me carry that? Just down the street? The Con-Ed's shut off our gas. My mother's got nothing to cook on."

"Carry what?"

"This." Tomás put a finger on the stove. "Look, I'll give you this yellow cloth."

The man looked at the cloth.

"I was gonna give it to my mother, but she'd rather have the stove," Tomás said.

The man smiled. "You keep that pretty silk, son."

He unwound the clothesline from around the stove and handed it to Tomás. He lifted the two-burner kerosene stove to his shoulders as though it were an empty bushel basket.

"Where do you live?" he asked.

"Just down a couple of blocks." Tomás wadded the cloth into a bundle, tied it with the clothesline, and led the way.

In the time it took to walk the five blocks home, Tomás figured out what to tell the man.

"We live on the top floor," he said apologetically.

"I guess you know kerosene stoves is against the law," the man said.

Tomás nodded. "The landlord's coming for the rent. I guess he shouldn't see the stove."

The man shook his head. "Unh-unh!"

"Could you put it on the roof? He won't go up there."

The man chuckled. "You are a right smart boy, son! When you grow up, your mama won't have to worry about no Con Eds and no landlord, neither."

He carried the little stove all the way to the top of

the building and out onto the roof. "You be careful, first time you light that," he warned. "It's liable to smoke like the old devil." He refused to take the yellow cloth. He refused the dime, too.

"Thanks, mister," Tomás said, "Thanks a lot."

"Glad to help," he said.

First, Tomás took the cloth down to Fernanda, and then the can that held kerosene and fitted on the end of the stove. Last of all, he tied the clothesline around the stove itself and lowered it over the edge of the roof like a crane unloading cargo. Fernanda helped him lift it through the window.

6

BEWARE! THE WATCHMAN

The next morning Tomás was crossing the roof with a gallon jug of kerosene he'd just bought at a service station on Chambers Street. He and Fernanda had been hiding for nearly a week now, and he had been going back and forth across the roof so often that he felt safe. He had grown careless, not bothering to check the blind windows across the back court or the other rooftops before showing himself.

Instead, thinking of lighting the new stove, he began to whistle. Fernanda could heat water to wash their clothes. He might even take a bath. He could pour a bucketful of hot water into the square iron washtub which stood on legs next to the sink and bathe in it.

"Hey, you—git off there!"

Tomás jumped. His whistle died in a gasp. He felt as conspicuous as a cat crossing an empty street. As he turned to hurry back toward the apartment house, he stumbled and the bottle of kerosene slipped from his hand. It fell on the tarpaper roof with a clunk. He bent to pick it up. The hot roof . . . the sun . . . the kerosene! What if the bottle was broken?

When he straightened up, the bottle again safe in his hands and unbroken, he dared to see who was shouting. He saw a man in a white shirt on one of the roofs across the court. The Market watchman!

Tomás knew him by sight—a small, mean-faced young man. His blue car could be seen cruising the streets on Friday and Saturday nights. He guarded the brown paper bags of potatoes stacked on the sidewalks, the red and white and purple bags of onions. He knew who belonged on the streets and who did not.

Tomás scurried back to the adjoining roof. He ran away from the hideout the way a meadowlark leads people away from her nest. No time to warn Fernanda. He hoped she had heard the watchman's shout and would have sense enough to take everything to the cave room and lock the door.

Quietly he opened the metal-covered roof door and stepped inside. He stood panting, trying to quiet his pounding heart. He still held the jug, which was dangerous. To get caught with kerosene would demand all sorts of explanations. He must get rid of it. But where? If he put it outside someone's door, it might get taken and he would lose fifty cents' worth of good kerosene.

He opened the door cautiously and peeked out. The watchman no longer stood on the other roof. Tomás knew the man could not cross over to the roofs on his side of the block. He would have to go downstairs and drive or walk around to this building.

Tomás stepped out onto the roof and looked for something to climb on. He found a backless chair, weathered gray. He set it next to the chimney. Carrying the bottle in both hands, he stepped up on the chair and set the bottle down behind the chimney. Then he went back inside and walked downstairs. Tomás peered out the open front door. The watchman had seen him. What now? He wanted to run away to where the watchman did not watch. But that was impossible. He had to guard the hideout and Fernanda.

A block away, the car slid into the empty street and rolled toward him. Tomás pretended to be looking for something in a garbage can.

The blue car pulled to the curb. The door slammed. Tomás was afraid to look, but he knew he must. He had to act as though he had nothing to hide, as though he had a clear conscience.

The watchman came toward him with long strides. When he spoke, his voice was angry. "What were you doing up on the roof?"

Tomás made his eyes big and innocent. *"No comprendo."*

The man's face turned pink. "Don't give me that!" he shouted. "You speak English. What were you doing up there?"

Tomás hung his head. "Nothing."

"Nothing! You know you can get shot walking around on roofs? That's private property. What were you looking for? Something to steal?"

"No!" Tomás became indignant.

"What were you doing, then?"

"Nothing!"

"You were carrying something."

Tomás struggled to think of something safe he might have been carrying.

"I had a book! And—and a jug of water."

The man snorted.

"It's true," Tomás cried. "I was looking for a place to sit and read. Without somebody always bothering me."

"Find some other place," the watchman ordered. "You won't find it so quiet getting shot at." He turned away and headed back to his car.

Harry, the garlic man, rose suddenly from a steel door in the sidewalk. The door led down steep steps to a basement. There, the garlic that arrived in big wicker baskets was poured onto a moving belt, and as the garlic bulbs rode along, workers picked them off and popped them, two by two, into neat little boxes which said *HARRY'S SELECTED GARLIC* on each end. Harry was skinny and flat-chested in his white apron. He waved at the watchman, and the watchman waved back.

Tomás's face grew hot. He hated the watchman. Look at him, waving like he was nice and friendly, when he wasn't. He was mean. He couldn't shoot. He wasn't even wearing a gun.

The car drove away, and Tomás kicked the garbage can. Then he dived into the hall and flew upstairs. From now on he would have to be more careful. He hoped Papa would not stay away much longer.

He picked up the kerosene jug and ran with it across the roofs and down the fire escape. He made sure he reached the hideout before the watchman could get back to the roof and catch him.

Sure enough, Fernanda had heard the shout and had locked herself in the cave room. When Tomás called, she opened the door a crack and looked at him fearfully.

"What happened? Who shouted?"

"Let me in," he whispered, panting.

He slipped gratefully into the safe, half-dark cave room, and she bolted the door behind him. He wiped his forehead with his sleeve and sank onto her bed, now covered, like his, with the silky yellow cloth.

"The watchman saw me," he began. "I'm glad you hid. That's what you're supposed to do."

He told her how the watchman had shouted and what he had said.

"I'm staying in the rest of today."

After a while when Tomás was sure it was safe, they

ventured back to the kitchen, keeping well away from the open windows.

Thoughtfully, Tomás said, "I wish I knew why he was up there. Then I'd know if he'll be going back."

He peeled a banana and began to eat it. "Until now we were only hiding from the Malloys and Welfare, but now I got somebody else to hide from—the watchman."

"But we have a stove," Fernanda reminded him. "That will make things better. Let's try it."

"No!" Tomás shook his head violently. "It might smoke at first. Do you want the fire engines to come?"

"Oh, you're so bossy!" she complained, walking away.

A soft rain began drifting out of the sky. Tomás watched it sifting against the black shutters opposite them.

"It's a good day to stay in," he said in his friendliest voice.

Fernanda went to the cave and came back with the new magazine and her scrapbooks. She spread a layer of newspapers on the floor. Tomás mixed a fresh batch of flour-and-water paste, and they played the magazine game.

They looked at each page, studied all the pictures, and read the ads. Fernanda coaxed him to read the stories aloud.

When they grew hungry at midday, they ate more bananas. Fernanda made a salad with two kinds of lettuce, tomato, cucumber, oil, and lemon juice. Except for the bowl, it looked like one shown in the magazine. Tomás had found everything except the oil.

He had worked hard Friday morning to find enough food to last the weekend, for he knew that by Friday night the big, round brooms of the sanitation machines would have scoured the streets bare of food.

Tomás and Fernanda carefully carried the stove into the light, and admired it—front, side, top, back. A metal plate screwed to the back told how to light it.

The rain had stopped as quietly as it began, but darkness came early. As the light faded, Tomás felt safer: at night the watchman guarded the onions and potatoes down on the street.

Tomás sat in one of the windows, watching the night arrive. And listening to it. From somewhere came a slow drip. Across the court he heard pigeons gargling in a nest behind an iron shutter.

Fernanda stood beside him.

"Soon now?" she asked.

"As soon as it's too dark to see smoke."

"*Mira*. Look!" She pointed. Two floors below, a rat ran along a big pipe and scuttled through a tin gutter at the edge of a roof. It drank from a puddle of water and returned the way it came.

Fernanda said, "You forgot to get a cat."

"It's not so easy," Tomás said in his own defense. "You think I can just stand in the street and call kitty, kitty, kitty, and cats will come running? Hah, if it's so easy, *you* do it."

"Maybe I will," she replied.

"Hah!" Tomás said again.

They watched darkness cover the buildings. "If we were sitting on the roof, we could see the river," Tomás said.

"But what if someone saw us?"

"They can't now. It's too dark."

Fernanda was silent a moment. "I'll go," she said.

"What?" Tomás could not believe his ears.

"I mean I might go," she said. "If you'll stay beside me."

"Sure!" He jumped up. "Come on."

They sat with their backs against a chimney.

"Boy, it would take a whole army of helicopters to see us," Tomás bragged.

"So that's the river," Fernanda said. "I was too frightened to look when I first came. It looks nearby and far away at the same time."

"I know. It's because this side *is* close, and that side is 'way over in New Jersey," Tomás explained.

They could see the Statue of Liberty holding her light, but the river lay as gray and empty as the Market's cobblestone streets.

"The ships have all gone home now," Tomás said. "You should see it in the daytime. Ferries and tugboats and barges and *big* ships, bigger than this whole block. And overhead an old helicopter goes whirring and whirring. It has a propeller at the back and one at the front."

At last Tomás decided it was dark enough to light the stove. They went back inside and by candlelight he reread the instructions. Tomás turned the handle that let the kerosene run from the tank to the burner. Then he waited, as the instructions directed. When he thought it was long enough, he turned the lever that raised the tin chimney and allowed him to light the wick.

"Stand back," he ordered Fernanda as he held the match to it. The flame caught and crept around the whole circle of the wick. He lowered the chimney back into place, and through the little isinglass window he watched the flame turn from yellow to blue. He put his hand over the burner but drew it back quickly.

"It's hot!" he said.

On one burner they put a pan of water, on the other a bucket of water, and took turns sticking a finger into the water to see how hot it was getting. Soon the water in the pan began to boil.

"Let's cook something," Tomás said.

"We haven't had supper yet," Fernanda remembered.

"Fried eggs," Tomás said dreamily. "Fried eggs and potatoes. Could you fry potatoes, the way they do in the luncheonette?"

"I could fry bananas," Fernanda suggested.

"Yes!"

When Fernanda put the food on the table, Tomás sat down on his crate, leaned back against the wall, and looked around with a happy sigh. He sniffed the food expectantly.

Fernanda sat down and Tomás took a big bite of banana. "Won't Papa be surprised?" he said with his mouth full.

70

Fernanda looked up from her plate. "What if he isn't coming back?"

"He *is* coming back!" Tomás shouted, and then clapped his hand over his mouth, remembering it was not safe to make so much noise. "Well, he is," he said more quietly.

Fernanda said nothing.

After supper, she washed the dishes in hot water. She had become used to working by candlelight. They heated more water, and Tomás took a bath. Then he went to bed.

The rain began again. Tomás lay listening to the drops pattering on the tin window-coverings. He felt warm and clean and not the least bit hungry. What if Fernanda was right, and Papa did not come back?

They would live here forever, just like this.

7

SABERTOOTH

On Sunday morning when Tomás made his usual trip to the street, the air smelled cool and clean, and it was so clear that the city looked freshly washed. White gulls sunned themselves on the roofs of the dock buildings, and high up to the north a sprinkling of tame pigeons wheeled and flashed.

Tomás felt good. He took a deep breath before he started down the street toward the dump. It was always possible that he had overlooked something on Friday night.

He rummaged around among strips of carpet and found two magazines and a pretty tin box decorated with pictures of cookies. The cookies made him realize he was hungry.

Fernanda had said she was going to wash her hair. She will be sitting in the window, drying it, he thought. Somehow I'll sneak the pretty tin box in and, when she's not looking, put it on the table.

But when he got to their hideout, Fernanda was not

sitting in any of the windows. He put the box on the fire-escape landing, out of sight against the wall. Fernanda would not be able to see it unless she stuck her head out.

She must be in the kitchen, Tomás thought, and she was certainly being very quiet. But the kitchen was empty.

Strange, he thought. She must be in the cave.

"Fernanda," he called softly, and went to look.

The cave room had no furniture except the bed and a few clothes hanging on nails. No Fernanda. Her bed under its yellow spread was smooth.

"Fernanda," he called again, beginning to worry.

He tiptoed part way down the dark staircase, holding the bannister to keep from slipping on chunks of plaster. He could see the hall below. At least she had not fallen downstairs.

He returned to the kitchen and was standing in the middle of the room biting his lip, wondering what to do, when he heard a noise. He listened. *Someone* was down there. He stood where he was, absorbed in listening.

It *must* be Fernanda. He opened the hall door again, and went out to lean over the bannister.

"Fernanda?" he said in a loud whisper.

"Oh, Tomás!" He saw her now, coming up the stairs. She looked excited and happy.

"Tomás," she called again. *"Mira!"* She was cuddling

something in both hands. "Look!" she cried, holding her hands out to him.

It was a kitten.

He forgot how she had frightened him. He forgot to be angry.

"Where did you get it?" he asked, reaching for it.

Its round blue eyes stared at him.

"Here, you may hold it," Fernanda said, and put the kitten into his arms. Its orange fur felt soft. Inside its round body, the bones felt soft, too. It scratched at his shirt front, mewing angrily.

"Ah, look at its little claws." He chuckled. "Where did you get it?"

"Downstairs. Oh, isn't it a darling, Tomás!

"I was looking out the window," she said. "I saw a cat run along the ledge. Down there. It jumped through a window into our building. I took a little stew in my bowl and called her. I found her on the second floor. With this kitten! The kitten hid, but I got it. I gave the mother the stew. I will get the bowl later."

At that moment, with a *meow,* the mother cat walked into the room. She rubbed against Fernanda's leg, purring. She was gray and white, and the tip of her tail was crooked.

"Do you want your baby?" Fernanda asked. Taking the kitten from Tomás, she held it before the cat's nose. "If you want it, you'll have to live with us, too."

The cat rubbed its ear against Fernanda's hand. Satisfied that her kitten was safe, she crossed the room to the window, jumped onto the sunny sill, and began washing herself.

Fernanda set the kitten on the floor. It took three unsteady steps and began chasing its orange tail. Tomás could not keep from scooping it up.

"We'll keep them both!" he cried. "The mother can catch rats."

"We can name them," Fernanda said delightedly.

"Sure," Tomás said. "You can name the mother because she's a girl, and I will name the kitten. Okay?"

"Okay."

Tomás held the kitten at arm's length and growled at it. "We're cave dwellers, see? And this is our pet tiger cub. So I'm going to call it Sabertooth!"

Fernanda thought. "I would like to name the mother McCall."

"McCall?" Tomás hooted. "What kind of a name is that?"

"The name of a magazine," Fernanda reminded him. "A woman's magazine. For a woman cat."

Tomás began to giggle.

She pretended not to notice. She held her hand out to the cat. "McCall! Here, McCall!"

Tomás laughed so hard he had to cross his arms over his stomach.

The cat jumped from the window sill and again rubbed herself against Fernanda's leg.

Tomás stopped laughing.

He remembered the cookie tin and the two magazines and ran to fetch them.

Fernanda's cheeks went pink with pleasure. "Oh," she laughed, "here are so many things to enjoy I don't know where to start."

The cats were a wonderful addition to their lives. They made Tomás and Fernanda feel like a family. They kept Fernanda company when Tomás was away, and, having Sabertooth to play with, Tomás did not feel so restless when he had to stay indoors.

Tomás thought McCall must belong to one of the warehouses, but she seemed to go there only for extra meals. The rest of the time she remained in the hideout. She dozed on the window sill in the day and caught rats at night. Three mornings in a row she brought dead rats to Fernanda, and mistook Fernanda's gasps at the sight of them for sounds of delight. Tomás hoped she would run out of rats. He was the one who had to take them to the trash can.

8

FISH

On Wednesday of that week Tomás was out walking along his usual route after the Market had closed, swinging his mesh sack half filled with pimientos and dark green bell peppers. In the bottom was the can of milk he had bought earlier for Sabertooth.

As he rounded a corner, he came upon a woman sorting through a bushel of green beans. He had begun to know that other people besides himself fed their families from what the Market threw away.

"Want some beans, son?" the woman asked. "Help yourself."

She was grandmother-shaped, short and plump. Tomás's eyes came level with her shoulder. Against her light blue summer dress her arms and face gleamed as soft and brown as chocolate.

Tomás began picking out good beans and putting them in his sack.

"I'd like to get about a pound of these," his new friend said. "Then I'm going over to the Fish Market and get me some fish."

Tomás stopped picking out good beans. "You mean there's a place where they throw away fish?"

"Sure there is, honey." She tossed a last bean into her shopping bag. "I'm going there now. You come along if you want to. We'll both get us some fish, if it ain't too late."

"Okay!" Tomás did a jump and skip. How surprised Fernanda would be! And McCall! And Sabertooth!

"My name's Tomás," he said as they started off.

"Pleased to know you, Tomás," she said. "Mine's Edith."

They walked and walked down Greenwich Street a long way, and then turned left and walked uphill to Broadway and downhill toward another river. Tomás began to smell the fish.

"That there's the East River," Edith said. "Think you can find your way back home?"

"Oh yes!" Tomás said. "I am sure I can." He had a good sense of direction.

All the fish stores were closed. Edith looked in the clean pine boxes standing on the sidewalks, but the boxes held only heads and tails and skeletons of fish.

"Come on," Edith said. "We go see if we can find this man that wanted cabbage."

They found a little, wrinkled, dark man on the splintery wooden pier where the fishing boats docked. He was sitting beside four baskets of fish.

Along the edge of the pier and on the corrugated

tin roofs, seagulls stood. They were the biggest gulls Tomás had ever seen. On their spindly legs they looked twice as big as McCall. The white ones with yellow bills looked clean and neat. The gray ones looked scruffy, like city pigeons. Tomás wanted to shout and run at them to make them fly, but he was afraid to. They looked as though they might turn on him.

Edith put two cabbages and a bunch of bananas on the box beside the man, who immediately took fish from the baskets and laid them on newspaper. Each fish was about the size of the man's hand.

"This is Tomás," Edith said.

The man said, "Pleased to know you," and counted out twelve more fish onto another newspaper. Tomás offered his peppers in return. The man accepted two.

Walking back toward the subway, Edith said, "He works there, making boxes. He takes the rest of the fish up to Harlem later and sells 'em.

"That's where I'm going now," she added, stopping before the subway entrance. "Sure hope I see you around again. I got a grandson your age. Remember, Friday's the best day for fish, but Monday, Tuesday and Wednesday, they good, too."

" 'Bye, Edith. And thank you!" Tomás shouted. He hurried home, holding fast to the loosely wrapped newspaper package, and smiling over the thought of the unexpected feast he was bringing to Fernanda.

9

TRAPPED

On Friday morning Tomás woke to the sound of long-drawn hoots. Foghorns! The boats sounded lost.

Remembering he had a lot to do because it was Friday, he dressed and skipped into the kitchen. Fernanda was washing her face at the sink. He was surprised to see that the world outside the windows was gray and misty.

He took his turn at the sink. Fernanda spooned coffee into his cup and poured in hot water.

"I bet it's late," he worried. "I better hurry."

The foghorns called and called. *Bleep! Moo-oo-oo!* Toot-toot! . . . Groan! . . . Moan! . . . Rowr!

"They sound like a traffic jam calling for help!" Tomás laughed.

He gulped the last swallow of coffee, shouted good-bye, and sprang up the ladder. No need to worry about anyone seeing him this morning. He could hardly see from one roof to the next, the fog was so thick. It was like walking in a cloud.

When he reached the roof door of the Pérez's building, he received a surprise. The door did not open. He tried again. It was *locked*—locked on the inside. He remembered the big hook that had always dangled there. It took him no time at all to realize the spot he was in.

If he could open the door a crack, he thought, he could slide in a wire and raise the hook.

But the door fitted tightly. He braced himself and tugged, hoping the dry wood might give. Nothing happened.

He wanted to haul back and kick the door, but the tin would make a booming sound. Someone might come and ask what he was doing there.

I have to get downstairs, he thought. I've got to find our food for the weekend. Besides, he did not want to go back and be stuck in the kitchen all day. Staying inside might be all right for Fernanda, but he liked the noise and activity of the street, the loading and shouting and honking followed on Friday afternoon by the gradual clearing-out of everybody, leaving the streets to him.

But food was the important thing. He had not been hungry for a long time, and he did not wish to be again.

He stood looking around at the chimneys and walls lurking in the fog. He noticed the backless chair he had used before. He snapped his fingers. Jumping up on it, he managed to skin up on the next building. It was much higher than the one he had climbed from. He knew there were three other buildings the same height next to it. Their roofs were separated only by low walls. He walked along the back edge of the buildings, looking for a fire escape which came clear to the roof.

On the last roof stood a row of six potted plants. Tomás could not remember having seen them when he had explored here before. He wondered who they belonged to.

He was about to turn back when he thought of trying the door. Perhaps the owner of the plants had forgotten to lock it.

Walking lightly for fear his footsteps would be heard by someone underneath, he went and gave the handle a light tug. The metal door swung out to his grasp with a slight squeal. Though he had hoped it might open, its doing so astonished him. He paused, gathering courage to go downstairs. With luck he could make it to the street without anyone seeing him. If someone did see him, his story was simple: he was visiting his aunt. He had gone up on the roof. Someone had locked him out.

He took a deep breath, pulled the door softly shut behind him, and started down the dim stairway. At the foot of it there was another door. His heart sank. *That* one would be locked.

He turned the handle, expecting, if it opened, to find a hallway. What he saw made him close the door quickly. This was not another empty building. Some-one *lived* there. He opened it a crack to take a better look.

The room looked like a room from the magazines— *really* like one. It was big—almost the length of the building, with a skylight in the ceiling. In the long side wall was a fireplace filled with white flowers and dark green leaves. Not plastic flowers like Mrs. Malloy's. Real ones. He could see fallen petals on the deep red carpet. Two pink, curly couches faced each other across a low table on which sat a milkwhite bowl piled high with red apples, round pink radishes and long white ones.

Tomás stood, fascinated. His eyes went from the pictures on the walls to the plants and small trees planted in wooden tubs near the front windows. On the window sill sat a monkey-faced cat—a cat with big ears and bright blue eyes.

Tomás tiptoed along the wall toward a door that he thought must lead to the next flight of stairs. He put his hand on the doorknob, then paused for one more look around. Nearby was an archway. Whatever was behind it was closed off by shutter-doors. He hesitated. There was no sound anywhere. The muffling fog gave him a sense of being the only person in the whole build-ing, in the entire Market.

He walked swiftly to the shutter-doors and opened them an inch. He stepped in to get a better look. At first he thought the room was empty. Then he saw that the walls were hung with drawings of a boy—a boy fishing, a boy in a coonskin cap, a boy milking a cow. The pictures were pinned every which way, some on top of each other.

The cat followed him in and watched Tomás. It did not seem unfriendly, but Tomás did not speak to it.

The floor was bare and splintery and splattered with paint. On a metal-topped kitchen table by one window were fat tubes and little thin tubes, full ones, flattened ones, and some rolled up like empty toothpaste tubes. The center of the table was covered with smears and blobs of paint.

Tomás shook his head. What a mess!

In the far corner stood a wooden thing, something like a ladder, holding a square of stiff white paper which someone had smeared with blue on top and a lot of green in one corner. Two big lights stood near it on tall, thin legs.

He took a last look around. The room was brighter now. Outside the fog was lifting. He could see the shuttered windows of the building across the court. He had better go.

He started for the stairway in high spirits. Maybe he would come back some time. This place was interesting. He wondered who lived here.

He was about to open the door that led downstairs when he heard sounds on the other side. Someone was coming up the stairs and shifting a paper bag from one arm to the other.

"Come on, Omar," a woman's voice said. "Hurry up!"

There was no mistaking the scurry of feet. Omar was a dog.

Tomás stood where he was. It was too late to try to hide.

10

BARBARA RANSOME

The next moment, the door was opened. A lady with a big bag of groceries and a smooth tan dog came in. The dog immediately began to yap at Tomás. He took a step backwards.

"Hello!" the lady shouted above the yapping. "I see the man from the egg store let you in. Omar! Stop it!"

She gave the dog a firm nudge with her sandal, and he went bounding through the room, springing and yapping at the cat. The cat looked at the dog with disdain.

Tomás stood watching, bewildered and a little frightened.

The woman disappeared behind a screen. She put the paper bag down with a thud, and turned on a light.

Tomás thought of bolting out the door and down the stairs. But just then the lady put her head around the screen and asked, "Didn't anybody come with you?"

Tomás shook his head.

"Hungry?" She peeled a banana. "How about a snack before we start?"

She set a glass of orange soda and cookies on a round table beside the screen. "Sit down," she said, seating herself.

Tomás took a quick look at the door by which he had hoped to escape. The silly dog came sniffing at him.

"Don't mind Omar," the lady said.

Tomás sat down on the edge of the chair and took a long drink of soda. Over the rim of the glass he studied the girl.

A band of blue ribbon held her tan-colored hair out

of her eyes. Her eyes were blue and she was wearing a faded blue shirt and tan slacks. Her arms and face and sandaled feet were as brown as his.

"What's your name?" she asked, serious as a teacher.

"Tomás Angelito Lorca."

"Ah, Tomás." She nodded. *Yo me llamo Barbara. Qué edad tienes?* How old are you?"

"Eleven," he said. "You speak Spanish!"

"A little." She pushed the plate toward him. "Have a cookie."

He took one of the three thick, chocolate-covered cookies. He wanted to eat slowly, feeling his teeth sink through the layer of chocolate into marshmallow, but he dared not. As soon as she found out how he came to be here, she would throw him out and maybe call the police. He chewed rapidly, stuffing the last bite into his mouth with his left hand while he reached for the second cookie with his right.

"Don't choke," she cautioned. "I'm not in that much of a hurry. Did you come here all by yourself, or did someone bring you?"

He swallowed, washed down the cookie with a drink of soda, and said:

"The man from the egg store didn't let me up—" He watched her, alert for a scowl. "I came across the roof."

Her eyebrows arched. "The roof?" Not anger but curiosity was in her voice.

"I was visiting my aunt. In the other building." He

pointed. "I went up on the roof and somebody locked me out."

Her blue eyes opened a little wider, but she didn't sound excited. She hardly sounded interested. "Then you're not the child from the agency?"

He shook his head slowly, wishing he were.

"Good thing my door was open," she said. She glanced at a big clock on the wall. "Where is that boy?"

Tomás shrugged, and smiled a little wistfully.

"Never mind him," she said. "What are we going to do about you?"

"That's no trouble," he assured her. "All I have to do is go downstairs, and then up the stairs to my aunt's."

"I see." Barbara nodded. "I didn't know any children lived in the neighborhood." She gestured toward the last cookie. "You better have that before you go. Do you live with your aunt?"

He didn't want to say yes and he didn't want to say no, so he said, "Sometimes."

Barbara looked at the clock again. "If the other boy doesn't come, would you like to pose for me?"

Tomás looked puzzled. "Yes," he said, "but I don't know if I know how."

"I draw pictures—pictures for children's books."

Tomás nodded, but she saw that he still did not understand.

"You know—for books like the ones you have in school and in the library," she said.

She went to a bookcase and took out a thin, green-covered book. Opening it, she showed him a picture of a Chinese boy sailing a kite. Tomás remembered seeing a picture like it pinned to the wall in the bare room. He ran his hand over the page.

She closed the book and showed him the front cover. One line read *Pictures by Barbara Ransome.*

Tomás gave her a pleased look. "You want to draw pictures of me? They'd be in a book?"

"Yes."

"Does—" he faltered. "Does it cost anything?"

"Cost you?"

"Like a camera picture," he explained.

"No—" She turned to put the book away. "No, this is different. I pay you."

"Wow!" He jumped up, becoming alert and businesslike.

"It's hard work," she cautioned.

"I like hard work," he bragged, giving himself a brisk slap on the chest.

She looked at the clock again. "Can you come back this afternoon? I should certainly know by then whether the other boy is coming. If he does, I'll let you pose for me another day."

Tomás nodded and started for the door. With all the excitement, he had forgotten the many things he had to do—remove the hook at the top of the stairs, find food, and sneak in some more kerosene.

Barbara Ransome said, "Come back by way of the roof, if you want, or ring the doorbell downstairs."

"Okay!" He jumped noisily down the stairs, two at a time, all the way to the sidewalk. He could not believe he could be so lucky. That woman was going to pay him to draw his picture. It might even be in a schoolbook, though he could not imagine how this could be.

But if nothing else came of meeting Barbara Ransome, he would have two ways to come and go from the hideout—like some little animals that he had read about. They lived in the ground and had two or three holes to get in and out by. That's how it would be with him now.

He was so happy he began to run and to sing Mr. Malloy's favorite song:

> *If her eyes are blue as skies,*
> *That's Peggy O'Neil.*
> *If she's smiling all the while,*
> *That's Peggy O'Neil . . .*

Then he whistled the tune as he raced from one box of discarded vegetables to another. He'd learned to clean the vegetables with a pocket knife he had found in a junk pile. It made less food to carry upstairs and less garbage to carry down.

When he had enough vegetables and fruit, he bought kerosene at the service station and put the jug into a purple mesh bag. A gallon lasted a long time—more than a week.

Finally, he climbed the four flights of steps and unhooked the door. The sun was shining now and already the roof felt hot. No air stirred, not even up here.

He set the food and kerosene in the shade of the wall and set about unscrewing the big hook with his pocket knife. When it came loose, he stood holding it, wondering where to put it. It wasn't his, so he didn't feel right about throwing it away. At last he fastened it to a rusty TV antenna. No one, he said to himself, would trouble to put it back.

He scuttled over the wall and home.

Breathlessly, he told Fernanda about the locked door, about the unlocked door on the other roof, and the beautiful room. She made him describe the beautiful room twice.

"What a nice lady," he bubbled, waving his hands. "She's tall like a movie star and wears pants. And she's going to draw pictures of me. She puts them in books."

Fernanda looked wistful.

"If you'd go outside, you could come with me," Tomás suggested slyly.

"Maybe, someday," she said.

She had cooked rice with pimientos and tomatoes again.

"When are you going to get more fish?" she asked.

"Maybe today, if I have time. Wow, am I busy!" He counted on his fingers. "Go get fish. See if Mrs. Salvador or Mrs. Pérez wants a baby-sitter. Go work for that lady—I hope! Whew! I never worked so hard in my life." He drank off the juice left in his bowl. "Pretty soon, I'll buy us some meat."

Then he remembered the third chocolate-covered cookie still in his pocket. He hauled it out, crumpled and melting, and handed it to Fernanda.

"Is she nice—the Señora?" Fernanda asked, licking the chocolate with the tip of her tongue.

"I told you she was," he said.

"Pretty?"

Fernanda always asked such girl questions.

"So long, I got things to do," he said and stepped out onto the fire escape.

On the roof he kept a wary eye out for the watchman. Across the river, flat blue now, the huge clock said twelve. The fire siren down the street gave its noon wail.

No, the Salvadors and the Pérezes did not need him. Perhaps tomorrow.

He set off on the long walk to the Fulton Fish Market.

11

BARBARA TAKES PICTURES

An hour and a half later Tomás stood on the sidewalk before the lady's door. In one arm he held a bundle of fish which he had wrapped in many layers of newspaper. He pressed the bell. Above it a neat card said

Barbara Ransome

ILLUSTRATOR

He heard a faint shout. He stepped back and looked up. She leaned out a window and threw down a tightly-rolled piece of brown paper. It landed on the sidewalk. He picked it up and unrolled it. It became a paper bag with a key inside.

He unlocked the door, and started up the stairs. The lower floors were dusty and empty. She's like us, he thought. She lives in an empty building. She has a hide-out, too, because nobody could ever find her unless she wanted them to.

She was waiting at the top of the stairs. Omar yapped

twice, ran away, and came skittering back to sniff at Tomás's feet.

"Miss—" Tomás began, "Miss, did the boy come?"

"No, he didn't. You have the job."

Tomás gave her a wide smile.

"You can call me Barbara," she said. "What have you got there?"

"Fish," he said shyly. "You can have some."

"How nice! Thank you. What kind of fish?"

"Just *fish* fish, I guess." He began to unwrap it.

"Looks good," she said. She picked up a round, meaty chunk. "This is about enough for me and the cat. How much was it?"

At that moment the cat purred and rubbed against Tomás's leg. "Mrowr?" the cat asked.

"This is Owa," Barbara said. "He smells the fish."

"I never saw a cat like him," Tomás confessed.

"He's a Siamese cat. Aren't you, Owa?" She looked seriously at Tomás. "His full name in Siamese is Owa-Taygoo-Siam. Can you say that—fast?"

Tomás shrugged. "Owa Taygoo Siam," he said easily. Then he heard the words come back to him: *Oh, what a goose I am!* He began to laugh.

He told her about Sabertooth and McCall. After a name like Owa, McCall did not seem so crazy.

"How much was the fish?" Barbara asked again.

"It was free," he explained. "Over at the fish market they just put it on the sidewalk for people to take."

100

"The *Fulton* Fish Market? Have you been clear over there and back?"

"Yes."

"Suppose I put it all in the icebox for now—till you're ready to leave. I'll take some as a gift today, but after this you'll have to let me pay you."

"All right," Tomás said. "Maybe I could sell some to other people, too."

She agreed and then said, "Come on in the studio. Let's get to work." She went into the room with the pictures hanging every which way on the walls. Tomás followed. A camera lay on the table.

"I'm going to be drawing pictures of a farm boy," she explained. "So I'll take pictures of you, sitting or standing the way I tell you. Then I draw from the snapshots. That way you don't have to sit in one position for hours at a time.

She took a pair of faded blue overalls from one of the shelves. Handing them to him, she said, "Go in the other room and put these on. Take off your T-shirt and your shoes. I want you wearing just the overalls."

Tomás giggled with embarrassment, but he obeyed. The dog trotted after him.

Tomás peeled off his shirt and twitched it at Omar. "Hey, boy," he whispered.

With a joyous growl Omar sank his teeth into the shirt and pulled. Tomás, a little surprised and frightened, pulled, too. Something ripped. He loosed his

Before anyone noticed, the afternoon was over. Again Barbara paid him two dollars. She also let him borrow the book.

After dark, back in their cave room, Tomás built a fire and read Fernanda the story by candlelight. Rain drummed against the tin-covered windows. A few drops fell down the chimney to sizzle on the coals. McCall crouched by the fireplace and Sabertooth curled in Fernanda's lap. They felt very snug.

Next morning, clouds still hung low. Tomás went to see Barbara first thing. He found her on the roof, sitting on a stool, with a large drawing board on her knees. Omar saw him, barked, and then ran to him to be petted. Tomás picked him up, hugged him, and gave Barbara a big smile.

"Hello, Tomás."

She was drawing the gray, oily river, the gray, curly clouds, the black buildings along the edge.

He shivered, and wished the sun would shine. "When are you going to Puerto Rico?" he asked.

"Oh, not for a long time," she answered, keeping her eyes on her pencil. "Don't worry, we'll go to the beach first."

"Will your brother go to Puerto Rico, too?"

She glanced at him. "How did you know about my brother?"

"You were going to visit him one day."

125

hold, and Omar raced off with the shirt to the front of
the room.

Tomás stood wondering what to do. He had never
owned a dog. He had never even known a dog. Omar
was small, but his teeth looked sharp.

"Miss! I mean, Barbara!" he shouted. "Omar stole
my shirt."

"Go get it," she called. "Hurry up. I'm about ready."

Tomás started, then stopped, standing on one foot.

"I'm scared he'll bite me."

"Omar? He only bites old men."

Tomás had to laugh. He ran to the front of the room. Omar lay crouched over the shirt. He growled.

Tomás stopped in his tracks. "He's growling," he reported.

"Growl back!"

Tomás bent forward and snarled.

Leaving the shirt, Omar bounded toward him, barking. Tomás dodged around a chair. Omar followed. Tomás dived for the shirt, whipping it away just before Omar's teeth snapped together on empty air.

"I got it," he shouted, laughing, running back to the chair where the other clothes lay.

Omar, panting, watched him pull on the faded overalls.

These are crazy pants, Tomás thought. He had seen them in books and on TV. They were what you wore in the country.

He found Barbara waiting with the camera. She looked him over. "You'll do, I think. Get up on the platform. Sit down and relax while I fix the lights."

She brought the tall lights on legs and stood them in the middle of the floor and turned them on him. They were too bright to look at.

"All right." She stood in the middle of the room,

looking at him. "Pretend you're a farm boy. You're lying on your stomach in the grass."

Tomás obediently rolled on his stomach.

"No, not sleeping," she directed. "Hold your head up."

Tomás raised his head.

"Have you ever been to Central Park? Ever lain in the grass?" she asked.

"No!" Tomás giggled at the thought of such foolishness. "A bee might sting me." He squinted, trying to see her beyond the bright lights. "I could be lying on the roof, though, looking at the river."

"Do that. Fine! Stay that way."

He heard a click.

"Okay," she said. "Remember how you were lying. I want to get another picture in a minute." She began to count: "—three, four—" At the count of ten she opened a door in the back of the camera and ripped out a piece of paper. She looked at it closely and then handed it to Tomás.

"Hey!" he cried. "That's me!"

It was the first picture he'd seen of himself since he was a baby, not counting a class picture in which his head had been a blur the size of a pencil eraser.

"Let me have it a minute," Barbara said. "We have to coat it with this stuff or it will fade." She showed him a round metal tube with a felt strip down the side. She rubbed the felt over the picture, turning it shiny. "There, see? Now, it'll keep."

104

He went back to lying on his stomach, pretending to watch boats on the river. Then she had him sit cross-legged, with one arm around Omar. She took more pictures. She let him coat each picture as it came out of the camera until, thinking of Fernanda, he could not help exclaiming, "I wish I could have one!"

"You can. But not any of these. I need these to work from. I'll take one later that will be just for you. Right now, I want you to stand on one foot. Pretend you're walking along a narrow railing." She drew a chalk line across the platform. "There, that's the fence."

Tomás had to do it again and again. He began to sweat. "The lights are so hot!" he complained.

"I know." She pushed back a lock of hair from her own damp forehead. "But we have to have them. If it's not light, the camera can't see. I told you it was work."

"Yeah." He nodded wearily. "I don't mind," he added, stretching out along the edge òf the platform while she waited for the picture to develop itself. "I like to work. When I grow up, I'm going to work all the time."

"If you work as well as you do now, you'll be rich."

"I will?" Tomás sat up, giving her all his attention.

"*I* think so," Barbara was saying.

"You think I work good now?" he asked, wanting to be sure.

"Yes," she said, not looking up from putting a new film pack into the camera.

Tomás jumped up and ran to look out the open window to hide how pleased he felt. Outside he could not see far. The air was like mist, but hot and sticky.

"All right," she said. "That's enough for today. We've been working two hours."

Tomás leaned on the table, studying each picture again and again.

"Here," Barbara said, picking one out of the group. "This one's for you."

The picture, taken close up, showed his head and shoulders. His hair looked thick and black; his dark eyes, bright as a puppy's.

"Will you need it to draw from?" he asked worriedly.

"If I do, I'll borrow it back."

At the little table next to the kitchen they drank Cokes and ate more cookies. Tomás leaned back in his chair, letting his legs dangle.

"Did you live here last month?" he asked remembering the plants on the roof, which had not been there before.

She told him she had been visiting in Mexico for half a year.

"Who lived here then?"

"A friend of mine."

Crossing his fingers under the table, he asked the question he was afraid to ask: "Are you going to live here now?"

"Yes."

He leaned forward, set his soda bottle on the table, and leaned back again. "I'm glad." He smiled.

"Do you like it here?" he asked, thinking what a silly question that was. How could anyone not like it—with a dog and all these colors and a whole roof of your own.

"I like it all right," she said.

Tomás looked around the pretty room. One thing was missing. "Don't you have a TV?" he asked.

"No," she said, and he could tell from her voice that she did not want one.

"I'll pay you now." She was getting her purse from the kitchen. "I'm going to visit my brother. I haven't seen him since I got back."

She returned with a brown billfold. "Two hours . . . two dollars."

Tomás could scarcely believe his ears, but it was true. She was handing him two green bills.

"Gee," he shouted. "Wow! Thanks!" He started for the stairway to the roof.

"Hey, your fish! And your picture," she called.

He rushed back. He put the money deep in his pocket, took the wrapped fish in one hand and the photo in the other. He ran through the living room to the door, and turned to shout goodbye. She was still standing by the table.

She took a step forward. "Stop by next week—"

"Okay!" he called happily.

He shut the door after him and ran up the stairs. The roof door on its heavy spring slammed behind him. Slowly, cautiously, he went from roof to roof, one eye cocked for the watchman. The docks and the river had their Friday evening look, the Market, its Friday quiet. Perhaps *this* was the weekend Papa would come.

Meantime, he could hardly wait to show Fernanda the picture and the money.

12

FINDING THINGS

As often as he could find an excuse, Tomás visited Barbara. The long busy days lost themselves in one another. He and Fernanda ate less rice, more fresh vegetables. The fish, the vegetables and fruit, the cracked eggs and frankfurters he bought, all began to make a difference in the way the children looked. The sun in the back room helped, too. Fernanda's cheeks and lips turned pink. Her black eyes sparkled.

Tomás found more things to please her. One day he found a white saucepan with a red handle, only a little bit chipped. It delighted Fernanda. Another day, in Staple Street, he found a teakettle.

"It was just sitting in a doorway," he told her. "It probably leaks."

But it did not leak. Fernanda rubbed it till it shone.

From the dump up the street, he brought a chair one day, and a small table the next.

Fernanda still had some of the yellow silk material. She cut it into curtains to hang over the tin-covered windows in the cave room.

Tomás bought kerosene and candles and candy and oleo and eggs and coffee and soap, and even bread once in a while.

Everywhere he found things. He or Fernanda had only to wish for something, it seemed, and within a few days he would come across it, dumped somewhere, waiting for him. At times he almost thought they did have a godmother, a fairy godmother, but that was crazy—a story for second graders.

One day Fernanda glanced up from her scrapbook. "Look, here is a room with yellow curtains, just like ours." She studied the colored photograph. "These people have a big picture hanging between the yellow curtains."

"Barbara has big pictures on her walls," Tomás bragged. "Here—and here—and here!" He ran around the cave room, pointing, showing Fernanda where Barbara would have pictures if this were her room. "—and over the fireplace."

"We need a picture," Fernanda said.

Tomás leaned against the wall. "It's pretty dark in here for a picture."

Instead of replying, Fernanda walked to the wall where she wanted to hang the picture. She stood on tiptoe and reached as high as she could. "Look," she said, "there's a nail already in the wall."

Tomás dropped his shoulders. "I'll try."

Three days later he saw something square leaning

against an empty wooden cheese barrel. He went closer to see what it was and could hardly believe his eyes. It was a picture. A big one, with frame and glass and a wire to hang it by. He squatted down to look at it more closely. He wiped off some of the dirt. The glass wasn't the least bit cracked. Under the glass was a white cardboard frame, and inside that a brown one, and inside that—He rubbed more dirt away and saw a familiar face.

George Washington!

He clutched it quickly to him so that the two men who were passing should not see it. If they saw whose picture it was, they might take it away. He stole a look at the nearest doorways. But no, someone had put it carefully there for anyone who wanted it.

Tomás hid his basket of vegetables behind the big wooden barrel. Then he picked up George Washington, carried him in both arms, watching every step he took.

When at last he got the picture safely down the fire escape into the house, and on the table in front of Fernanda, he drew a deep breath. His arms ached, but he had brought it home without damaging it at all.

Fernanda liked the picture, especially its size and the white lacy scarf George Washington was wearing around his neck.

"Was this his market?" she asked, washing the glass.

Tomás was scornful. "He was a President. He didn't bother with markets."

Fernanda stood on a box and hooked the wire hanger over the nail, while Tomás stood back and made sure it hung straight.

Fernanda did not seem surprised that Tomás had found the picture. Tomás wondered if she thought the streets were filled with good things, there for the taking. Well, they were, of course. But there's work to it, too, he said to himself, going back downstairs to fetch the vegetables.

He went past the same spot again the next morning just for luck and saw something else on the loading dock—a long, dusty roll of paper, standing on end. He jumped up on the dock and unrolled it part way—far enough to see that it was a map.

Like at school, he thought excitedly. And like the school maps, it was fastened to round, black sticks at the top and bottom. He unrolled it a little more, cocked his head sideways, and read the row of square letters across the top, UNION PACIFIC RAILROAD. On one side it said, *Geographically correct map of the United States*. His heart gave a jump of excitement. I can teach Fernanda, he thought.

Quickly he re-rolled it, tucked it under his arm, and marched home. When you found a special treasure the first thing to do was to get it safely home. Otherwise somebody else might take it.

He found Fernanda elbow-deep in suds, washing one of her dresses and two of his T-shirts.

"Look," he called gleefully from the fire escape. "Look what I found today!"

"What?" She left the sink and stood watching while he put the roll on the clean-swept floor.

"A map!" He looked around for something heavy enough to hold the top end flat while he unrolled it.

"Wait, I know." Fernanda ran into the other room and returned with two bricks.

In his eagerness to see the whole thing Tomás unrolled the old paper too hastily. One edge began to tear away from the top stick.

"*Cuidado!*" Fernanda warned. "Careful! It's tearing."

The brittle, browned paper had already cracked in several places.

"Oh!" Tomás mourned. Kneeling, he fitted the crumbled edges together as if, put back in place, some magic would mend them.

"Never mind," Fernanda said soothingly. "I'll patch it on the back with paste and strips of paper. What's it a map of?" She walked around to where she could look down at some letters. "Gulf—of—Mex—" she began to read.

"Gulf of Mexico!" Tomás shouted. "It's a map of the United States. See, here's every state."

"Where's New York?"

"Here. See, here's where we are." He crawled back and forth. In the bottom corners smaller maps were set in. He crouched on knees and elbows, chin in hand. "'Atlantic Ocean and Principal Steamship Lines between Atlantic Ocean Ports,'" he read aloud. "Oh, boy! Here's where all those ships come from. Across there—" His finger followed dotted lines across the blue ocean between the continents and then moved quickly to the western corner, and to the Pacific.

"Where's Puerto Rico?" Fernanda asked.

"I know. Wait a minute." Tomás searched the small map of the Atlantic Ocean. "Cuba . . . Haiti . . . here— Puerto Rico."

"So small?"

"This is just a small map."

Sabertooth joined them. He walked curiously across the paper, sniffing, plopped down on the Great Lakes and licked his side.

"A monster!" Tomás cried, falling over backwards. "A monster is prowling across the country . . . from west to east. When, ladies and gentlemen, he gets to New York City, stay in your apartments. One lash of his tail will kill a thousand people!"

"One scratch of his claw will tear the map, too," Fernanda said matter-of-factly.

Tomás swooped up the cat. "Come on, Monster. You have to go back to Mars."

Together, Tomás and Fernanda mended the map and hung it on the wall above the table where they could study it during meals.

One hot, muggy Sunday two men cleaned out a whole building on Duane Street. They were dumping the last odds and ends on the sidewalk when Tomás rounded the corner. He watched them finish up and lock the door. He stood wide-eyed as they climbed into their car and drove away.

For a moment he couldn't move. Here was unbelievable treasure. It was so splendid he was unable to decide where to dig first. He walked around the edge. There was a brown leather couch, but it was so old the leather was crumbling to dust. It sent up a brown powder even when you touched it gently. There were two office desks but they were in pieces. Most of the boxes were filled with stacks of gray cardboard, dividers for egg cartons. They were spotted with yolk and bits of broken egg shell.

Next he came across a man's tan raincoat, with a big label inside that gave washing instructions. It had no rips; he laid it aside.

He dug in further, and found some books, which delighted him until he saw that the pages were covered with black squiggles instead of words. He laid one aside so that he could ask someone what it meant. He found some pads of blank paper and four unsharpened pencils, and then, opening a neat cardboard box, he came across a folded pink washcloth which looked and felt brand new. Underneath it lay a heavy paper-wrapped package. He tore open the wrapping.

116

It was a bolt of cloth. The pink roses and green leaves on a white background were so beautiful that he gave a low whistle. His eyes sparkled. What Fernanda could do with that! He unfolded a little of the cloth. There seemed to be yards of it. It was a good thing that Grandmama had taught Fernanda to sew.

"She can make herself about sixty dresses," he said.

With his usual caution he gathered up this treasure, put the cloth back in the box along with the pads, the pencils, the washcloth and the raincoat, and hurried home.

Until he reached the roof with his prizes he had been too busy to notice the dark clouds settling in low over the city. A spatter of rain fell as he made the fire-escape landing. While he was unpacking the box, it began to rain hard.

He and Fernanda lit a candle and sat looking at Tomás's marvelous finds and listening to the rain. Fernanda made a jar of lemonade from a lime and two lemons Tomás had found on Friday, and as they drank it, they talked about what Fernanda could make from the cloth of roses. A dress, of course. Maybe two. She could see herself in them. They would be beautiful.

"Oh dear!" she suddenly cried in dismay.

"What?" Tomás demanded.

"I have the needle, but I used up all the thread to make the curtains."

"That is nothing, Fernanda." Tomás waved his hand. "I will buy you some tomorrow."

117

"There is enough cloth for our whole family." She giggled. "I can make a dress for McCall and a tiny shirt for Sabertooth," she added as Sabertooth made a dive under a fold of the cloth.

"Would you like that?" she demanded of the kitten, pulling him out and holding him at arm's length above her head.

"I have an idea!" Tomás shouted. "Why don't you make something for Barbara?"

Fernanda stared at him, thrilled with the idea. "What could I make?" she asked slowly.

"A dress?"

"I don't know how big she is."

"A tablecloth, then."

Fernanda shook her head.

"A handkerchief!"

"No, silly." Fernanda took a sip of lemonade and put her chin in her hand. "I could make an apron, a pretty apron . . . with a ruffle. Look, I saw one in the new magazine. I'll show you."

She found the picture and shoved it under Tomás's nose.

"Could you make that?" he asked, impressed.

She nodded.

"Yes? Do it then. Maybe she'll like it so much, she'll let you come over and look at her house."

Fernanda sighed. "I'd like to see it."

"Oh, you'd like it, Fernanda," Tomás said. "It's

prettier than all those pictures together, because you can walk around and smell it and feel the pink couches, or touch anything you want to."

He looked at her from the corner of his eye.

Fernanda reached for one of the scrapbooks which happened to be lying on the table. She opened it. "I can walk around these rooms, too," she said, fingering the pictures. Her face took on a stubborn look.

Tomás wanted to shout, "You can NOT!" but he caught himself and stopped. Instead, he took the magazine with the apron picture and laid it on top of the open scrapbook.

"How soon could you make the apron?" he asked.

Fernanda thought for a moment. "Three days, maybe more."

"Would you go to Barbara's then—if she'd let you?"

Fernanda studied the picture of the apron. "I might."

Tomás sat on the floor beside all the good things. He swallowed the last of his lemonade and rocked back and forth, hugging himself. "Isn't it nice here? Haven't you had more fun since we've lived here, Fernanda?"

A shadow crossed her face, but she answered readily enough, *"Sí."*

However, when they sat down to supper that night, she picked up her fork and laid it down again. "Tomás, we have been here a long time."

"Yes," Tomás agreed. He had no idea how long. It is hard to keep track of time without a calendar. Without

119

school to tell him the day of the week, he had trouble enough knowing when Friday came round. Whether it was July or August made little difference. He supposed he would somehow know when school reopened.

"So what?" he asked finally.

"I do not think Papa is coming back."

Tomás felt a pain in the middle of his chest. It hurt so much for a minute that he could not speak. Then it went away, leaving him very sad. He missed Papa. Papa had sung a lot whenever he was home. Tomás felt so sad that the food made a lump in his throat, but he did not feel afraid.

"I will look out for us," he said. "Barbara says I work so hard that when I grow up, I will be rich." A sudden fear struck him. "Fernanda, don't you like it here?"

"*Si,* Tomasito. But we cannot *stay* here."

"Why not?"

"Winter will come. How will we keep warm?"

Tomás leaned back in the chair. "I'll think of something," he promised.

13

RAIN

As if to prove Fernanda's words, the next day the weather turned cool. As Tomás went about his chores, the problem settled in the back of his mind and bothered him: Papa is not coming back. What are we going to do?

For three days it rained. Fernanda cut off the bottom of the raincoat and shortened the sleeves. When Tomás wore it he fancied he looked like a spy on TV. Between downpours the sky stayed gray, the air damp. It seemed to him that summer had lasted a long while. It must be nearly school time. He went to ask Barbara.

"How did you know I wanted you?" she exclaimed when she opened the roof door.

"You want me to pose again?" he asked, pleased that he remembered the word.

"This time you're going to be a Puerto Rican boy— just like you. Except the boy in this story has just come to New York."

121

"I've never been to Puerto Rico," Tomás said.

"I haven't either," Barbara said. "But I may go there this winter. Come on in. I'll show you the pictures I drew of you."

As they went downstairs a wonderful idea struck Tomás. "Maybe I'll go, too!" He remembered a sign he'd passed on the way to school: *PUERTO RICO and back, $13.00*. "How much do you think it would cost to just *go* there?" he asked.

"About a hundred dollars," Barbara said. "Maybe a little less."

"A hundred dollars! No—" He told her about the sign.

When she explained that $13 was the down payment, and that you had to come back and pay the rest of the money, Tomás was stunned. But he didn't give up the idea entirely. It was still a good one. The problem was how.

Perhaps Barbara would take him along to pose. No, there were probably a thousand boys in Puerto Rico who would be glad to pose.

"Miss . . ." he began. "I mean, Barbara, is the summer over?"

"Looks like it, doesn't it?" she said cheerfully.

"I mean, is it time for school to start?"

She glanced at a calendar on the wall. "No, you have a whole month yet. Don't worry, it'll get hot again."

The picture she showed him was of a boy not wearing shoes.

122

"Doesn't he cut his feet, walking barefoot like that?" Tomás asked.

"Sometimes," she said, "but he doesn't mind. There —see—he's wearing a Band-Aid."

Then she took pictures of Tomás pretending to chase a chicken, and cutting sugar cane with a long knife.

After they had both worked hard for a long time, she put the camera away. "I have to show a boy swimming, too," she said. "I guess we should go to the beach for that." She looked at him, and the way she asked, "Do you like the beach?" made him feel she was teasing him.

"I don't know," he confessed.

Her eyes widened. "Haven't you ever been swimming?"

"Yes, a long time ago. When Raimundo and his sister lived here, we went sometimes to the pool at Carmine Street."

"I guess we'd better take you to the beach, then."

"When?"

"Not today. It's supposed to rain again. How about next week?"

"Yes!" He spun around on one heel. "Oh!" His face fell. "I don't have a bathing suit any more."

"We can fix that," she said, and looked up as raindrops pelted against the skylight.

"You'd better wait here till it stops," she told him. "You don't want to get wet. Besides, you might slip on the roof and fall."

Tomás agreed to wait.

Barbara gave him a peanut butter and jelly sandwich, a glass of milk, and a book to read. She ate while she worked at her drawing board.

She had put down an old rug under the window where he could lie while he read and ate. He pretended it was a raft. Omar swam across the floor to join him. Tomás pulled him aboard. Owa the Siamese found a sheet of drawing paper and curled himself up on a raft of his own.

"So I was. No, he's too busy."

"Does he draw pictures, too?"

She shook her head. "No, he's a doctor. A special doctor—a psychiatrist. People go to him if they feel unhappy or afraid, and he helps them."

"Afraid?"

"Well, yes, afraid of things they shouldn't be afraid of. Things most people aren't afraid of."

"Like the Market watchman? *People* aren't afraid of him—but I am."

She did not look up from the drawing board. "Not quite like that. Maybe you have reason to be afraid of him—"

"He doesn't like me," Tomás said with a shrug.

"Anyhow, that's not the kind of fear I mean. I mean people whose fears keep them from living a normal happy life. You probably don't even know anyone like that."

Tomás did not answer. He was thinking of Fernanda. Perhaps that was the kind of being afraid that Barbara meant.

He said, "Like if somebody was afraid to go outside and never went out of their apartment?"

"Yes." She looked at him in surprise. "Do you know someone like that?"

"Yes. Someone. How could your brother help them?"

"Well, it would depend—on how old the person was,

126

and on other things. Who do you know who's afraid to go out?"

"This girl. She's fourteen. Could he make her not be afraid to go outside?"

She thought a minute and then said, "My brother's coming for lunch tomorrow. You could ask him."

Tomás looked to see if she meant it, and decided she did. He hugged himself suddenly and rolled his eyes. "I'd be scared to talk to him!"

"Tomás . . . do you realize we've been friends for three weeks, and I don't know the first thing about you —where you live, how many brothers and sisters you have."

"I live with my aunt."

"I thought you were just visiting."

"I live there this summer."

"Who's the girl who's afraid to go out?" Barbara asked.

"Just a girl."

"Has a doctor ever been to see her? An ordinary doctor?"

Tomás shook his head. "She isn't sick."

Barbara said, "You'd better have lunch with us tomorrow and talk to my brother."

Tomás drew a deep breath. "Okay." For Fernanda he would do it.

14

A TRIP TO THE BEACH

Next morning the sun was already hot when Tomás crossed the roof. The city steamed. He could barely see the Statue of Liberty.

"Hi, Tomás," Barbara greeted him. "My brother just called. He's not coming today. Let's go to the beach."

The beach! And not to have to talk to the doctor. He felt doubly glad.

"Go ask your aunt." Tomás started off. "And hurry. It's a long drive."

"Drive?" he echoed. He felt his smile stretching. "Do you have a car?"

"You'll like my car," she promised. "Go ask and hurry back. Tell her I'm taking you to Far Rockaway."

He ran first to tell Fernanda. "I'm going to the beach," he shouted, jumping in through the fire-escape window.

"Where?"

"The beach! It's called Far Rockaway."

Fernanda's eyes widened with fear. "When will you come back?"

"Tonight, silly! I'm going with Barbara. In a car. Goodbye! I have to hurry." He scrambled out the window again, but before climbing the ladder he turned and put his head back into the room. "I'll bring you something nice, Fernanda," he promised. "Maybe candy."

He clambered up the ladder, ran across the roofs, and tiptoed down the stairs to the Pérez apartment. He knocked on the door.

He wished he had never taken up baby-sitting. He visited Mrs. Pérez and Mrs. Salvador every morning, but he worried that one day one of them would go to his old building, looking for him. If that happened, Mrs. Malloy would tell Mr. Malloy, "Tomás is not in Brooklyn. We must get to the bottom of this." And she would.

"I cannot baby-sit today," he said when Mrs. Pérez opened the door. "I am going to the beach."

"*Sí*, that is nice. I will tell Mrs. Salvador. Have a good time."

He ran on down the stairs, his sneakers just touching the edges. He went to Barbara's street door and rang the bell.

She opened the window. "In a minute," she shouted.

She came down carrying a basket and a blue bag with white rope handles. The camera in its brown case was swinging from a strap around her neck.

She had tied a red-and-white bandanna over her hair.

She was wearing a red-and-white shirt to match, and white shorts and sandals.

"You look just like a magazine!" Tomás shouted.

A man walking past turned and winked at him.

When Tomás looked back at Barbara, he saw a dimple disappearing in her cheek.

She handed him the blue bag. "This way." She started off up the street, and Tomás had to run to catch up.

When they passed his old apartment house, he held his breath. Mrs. Malloy might be looking out the window. He tried to walk close beside Barbara so that anyone seeing them would think he was her little boy. He saw no one, but he felt better when a truck that was backed on the sidewalk hid them from view.

Outside the garage in the next block they had to wait while a man brought the car down on an elevator. It was a bright red car with no top.

"That's it," Barbara said.

"Honest? I get to ride in that? Yippee!" He spun around on his heel.

Barbara put the basket, the blue bag, and the camera on the back seat. Tomás sat in front beside her. Then they were rolling down Greenwich Street between parked trucks. He leaned back against the red leather seat and looked up at the familiar buildings. His chest swelled. He took a deep breath and tried to sit still, but he was too excited.

Barbara glanced sideways at him. "Like it?"

"It's like a parade!" He laughed, bouncing on the seat. He hoped everyone would see him. Except Mrs. Malloy. He wished Fernanda could see him. He looked up to the roof, wanting to wave.

"The first stop is to get you a swim suit," Barbara said. "I guess Canal Street would be good."

On Canal Street they passed a clothing store. Barbara turned the corner and stopped. "I can't park," she explained. "Too much traffic. Here—" She took two dollars from her billfold. "You pick out some trunks. Ask the clerk your size. I'll stay with the car."

"Okay!" he cried. Clutching the two bills, he ran around the corner and into the store.

A man showed him a stack of swim trunks his size. Tomás chose red ones. He ran back to the counter with them, and jumped from one foot to the other while the clerk wrapped a set of lace curtains for a woman.

"What's your hurry?" the man teased, putting the trunks in a bag. "The beach won't wash away."

Tomás giggled.

"Okay," the man said, "here's your change. I hope the ocean doesn't dry up before you get there."

Back in the car, Barbara took the trunks from the bag and held them against him. "I guess they'll fit."

She put the change back in her purse, and Tomás carefully took the price tag off his trunks.

"We're off!" she said. Tomás thought her voice sounded happy.

"Are you going to swim?" he asked.

"Yes, of course. Aren't you?"

"Do I have to?"

"No. You can play in the sand, or do whatever you like."

"Is there sand?"

"On the beach? Sure. Lots of it. There's sand and lots of people and beach umbrellas and towels and everything you could want—including a basket of food."

Tomás sat in a blissful daze while the car crawled through the traffic. Suddenly they dipped into a tunnel and the air began to smell strange and choking.

"Do you like breathing here?" he shouted above the roar of wind and tires.

"Terrible!" she shouted back.

He tried holding his breath, but the tunnel went on and on. He began to wonder if it ran the whole way. Going to the beach was not so much fun after all.

Suddenly they came up into fresh air and slowed down. The other cars were forming lines leading to toll-collection booths. Barbara moved her car into line too. When their turn came, she handed the tollhouse man a coin.

"Is this the beach?" Tomás asked.

Barbara shook her head. "No. We pay to use the parkway. We're just getting started."

15

FAR ROCKAWAY

They drove and drove, among hundreds of cars. On the other side hundreds more went whizzing by going toward the city. They drove on a highway built above the street and then along the edge of the water. Barbara said that all that smooth water disappearing into the haze was part of New York's harbor.

After a long time she drove into a parking lot. Tomás saw nothing but buildings. "Where's the water?" he asked.

Barbara was taking things out of the car. "Over there," she said, tossing her head in the direction of the ocean and handing him the beach bag.

Suddenly as they turned a corner at the end of a street, there was the ocean.

"Is that it?" He danced along.

"That's it."

"When can I put on my suit?"

She stopped at a hot dog stand and rented a blue umbrella, the biggest umbrella Tomás had ever seen.

There was nothing but sand between a row of houses and the water. People were scattered all along the beach, lying on blankets and towels, in the sun or in the shade of umbrellas. Children of all sizes were running, shouting, wading, digging.

Tomás followed Barbara, sinking into sand at every step.

"Can I take off my shoes?" he asked.

"In a minute." She led the way to an unoccupied place on the sand about halfway down to the water.

"How about setting our umbrella up here? The tide's coming in. If we go closer, it'll chase us back in no time."

He looked around at the people near them. Some had chairs and tables.

"Do they live here?"

"No. They've come to spend the day and want to be comfortable."

She opened the umbrella, so that it rested on the sand. "First, we'll make you a little dressing room." She took a big bathtowel from the top of the basket and draped it across one half of the open umbrella. "There, put your suit on in there."

He took the red trunks from the bag and pulled them on in a hurry.

"Do they fit?" she asked from the other side of the towel.

"I guess so." He strutted into the sun.

"They look fine," she said. "You did a good job of picking them out."

"I buy lots of things," he boasted. "Rice and bread and eggs and magazines and candles."

"Candles?"

"I only buy candles sometimes," he said, wishing he had not mentioned them, but she was busy working the umbrella pole deep into the sand.

"Where's your suit?" he asked.

"I'm wearing it." She unbuttoned her shirt and Tomás saw a yellow swim suit underneath.

She put the camera in the basket and covered it with a towel.

"Ready?" She held out her hand to Tomás.

Together they ran across the sand to where it dipped smooth, wet, and shiny down to the waves.

At the water's edge, he pulled back. Barbara let go of his hand, leaving him feeling both glad and sorry. Underfoot the wet, dark sand almost tickled, it felt so smooth and firm. Every place he stepped the water made a silvery footprint.

He watched a wave flow back into the sea, leaving a tiny white shell. He ran to pick it up, holding it for her to see.

"Look, a shell!"

The next instant the wave caught him, boiling coldly over his feet.

"Agh!" he shouted, leaping out of its way. And

suddenly Barbara was laughing at him. He began to laugh, too.

"It caught me!" he screeched, running down to the water's edge and giving it a kick. It turned and came back. He ran from it, shrieking.

Soon he became used to waves coming and going. He ran whooping and splashing, first along the edge, then dared to go deeper until the water foamed around his knees. Barbara watched him for a while, and then swam out beyond the breaking waves. He could see her yellow bathing cap bobbing beyond the green walls of water.

He poked along the water's edge, looking at bits of glass and pebbles made smooth by the sand and water. He noticed the different kinds and sizes of shells. He picked up the prettiest and the unbroken ones until both hands were full and he had to run back to the umbrella to dump them down beside the basket. He would take these as a present to Fernanda. He went back to gather more.

Barbara came riding in on a wave and waded out of the water, breathless and dripping.

Together they went back to the cool sand under the umbrella. She spread a striped towel for each of them. Lying on his stomach, face propped in his hands, Tomás watched a tiny girl shovel sand into a pink bucket. When the bucket was full, she carried it down to the water and dumped it in.

"How far down does the sand go?" he asked, worrying that perhaps careless children might carry it all away.

"I don't know." Barbara sounded puzzled. "I suppose it goes down a long way."

"Deeper than I could dig?" he asked, working his fingers into it.

"Oh, yes."

"Who put it here?"

"Who? Why, the ocean. The water grinds and grinds against big rocks for thousands of years. It wears them down to these minute particles that we call sand."

Barbara spread sunburn lotion over his face and back and gave him the bottle so that he could put it on his arms and legs and chest himself.

Far out he saw three small white boats.

"What are those boats doing out there?" he asked.

"Fishing," she said.

"Could you swim that far out?" Tomás asked.

"No," she said, "not half that far."

Tomás ran off to wade again, and, after that, they ate sandwiches and shared a banana and drank soda. Then Barbara made him lie in the shade and rest.

The wind felt exactly right. His skin felt dry and tight. He thought of Fernanda and sighed. If only she were here, everything would be perfect. I have to talk to the doctor, no matter how scared I am, he told himself.

And then he was asleep.

16

BACK TO MANHATTAN

When he awoke, Barbara was wearing black sunglasses and drawing on a pad propped on her knees. He reached out and patted her bare foot. The sunglasses turned toward him.

"Hi! Have a nice nap?" she asked.

He smiled and lay looking out at the sparkling sand and sea. He wished he could live here forever, except when it snowed.

He sat up.

"Would you drive your car to Puerto Rico?"

"Most of the way, yes. What made you think of that?"

"It's always warm in Puerto Rico. If you go, would you take me with you?" If she would take me, he thought, I can coax her to take Fernanda, too.

"Wouldn't your mother miss you?" The black sunglasses turned his way, then back to the child she was drawing.

"I don't have any mother."

"Oh? I didn't know that, Tomás." She stopped sketching to talk. "What about your father?"

Tomás shrugged. "He doesn't come home so often."

"You *live* with your aunt, then," she said. "You're *not* just visiting."

"It's a very long visit, and I think perhaps she is growing tired of me—of us—my sister and me."

"Is your sister the one who's afraid to go outside?"

"Yes. Fernanda."

"What about school?"

Tomás shrugged again and threw out his hands, shoulder high. "There are schools in Puerto Rico."

"How can Fernanda go to Puerto Rico if she's afraid to go outside?"

"Your brother could cure her!" Tomás had his plans all worked out. "Your brother could cure her, and I'll bring fish and vegetables to eat, so you can save money for gas, and I'll save some money, too, and when we have enough, we'll go."

"Well, that certainly sounds ingenious, Tomás."

"What's that mean?"

"Clever. Well thought out. But I'm afraid it's not that simple."

"Why not?" Grownups always made things hard.

"For one thing, it takes more money than we could save on just fish and vegetables. And we don't know if my brother can do anything to help Fernanda. But I'll speak to him and maybe he'll come to see her. And right now we have to start for home. What time are they expecting you?"

"They don't care," Tomás said.

Briskly, Barbara began to gather their things. "It'll be growing cool soon, and besides we have to get home before the rush hour traffic starts, though luckily most of it will be going the other way. Is your suit dry?"

Tomás felt it and nodded.

"You can put your clothes right on over it then," she said.

The ride back was long. The sun, also heading westward, shone right in Tomás's eyes.

When at last they crossed a bridge, Barbara said, "We're back in Manhattan."

Tomás felt glad.

They left the car at the garage and walked home. As they came to Barbara's building, they saw a man standing at the door. He had thick white hair and wore a light suit. He looked hot, but not cross.

"Charles!" Barbara cried.

He greeted her with a smile. "Hello, Barbie."

"How long have you been here?" she asked. "You should have called. I might have missed you!"

The man kissed her cheek and took the basket. "But you see, you didn't miss me," he said smiling. "I had to come downtown on business, so when I finished, I took a chance and came over. Do you know, it's five degrees cooler down here?"

Tomás stood there feeling left out. At last Barbara turned to him. "That's why we live here, isn't it, Tomás?" she said lightly. He felt her hand on his shoulder. "Tomás, this is my brother."

"How are you, Tomás?"

Tomás scowled. "Okay."

Barbara took the blue bag from Tomás's hands. " 'Bye, Tomás. I'll see you tomorrow," she said to him. She turned back to her brother. "Are you as thirsty as I am?" Tomás heard her ask as she unlocked the street door.

He did not hear what the doctor answered because they went inside, and the door slammed and locked itself behind them.

Too late Tomás remembered that the shells, seaweed, and pebbles for Fernanda were in the bottom of the blue bag.

Going up the stairs of the Pérez and Salvador tenement, Tomás decided to go and knock on Barbara's roof door and ask for the shells. Perhaps she would give him a cold drink, too. After all, she had promised to let him talk to the doctor, although now he didn't know whether he wanted to or not. He was probably all right, her brother, but Tomás hoped he wouldn't come visiting often.

Tomás reached Barbara's roof and made his way

across to the open skylight directly over the kitchen. Below, the refrigerator door slammed. An ice tray thudded in the sink. There was the sound of running water followed by ice cubes clinking into a bowl.

"Charles?" He heard Barbara call. "Charles, what about people who are afraid to go outside? Are they hard to cure?"

She was out of sight, but right below Tomás, at the table.

"Depends on the cause."

"What about a child?"

"How old?"

"Fourteen, I think."

Tomás leaned down close to the open skylight.

"All disturbances are easier to cure in children. Is it someone you know?" the doctor was saying.

"Yes. Tomás's sister, Fernanda."

There was a silence and then Barbara said, "It's the usual story, I guess. Tomás doesn't give out with much, but I gather the mother's dead, and the father· doesn't often come home. They seem to live with an aunt. Today he asked if I'd take him to Puerto Rico with me. And his sister."

Her voice sounded amused.

The sound of her voice made a lump form in Tomás's throat and then go away when she added, "Maybe I will."

He heard quick footsteps, the doctor's, walking from

the living room rug across the bare floor to the kitchen. "You're not serious," he said.

"Yes, I am."

"Saddling yourself with two kids?"

"Why not?" Barbara asked.

"What for?" the doctor said. "Children are bad enough when they're your own, but somebody else's . . . ?"

Barbara's answer reached Tomás clearly. "I suppose you're right. You always are. Take your glass. Let's sit in the living room."

Tomás tiptoed away.

It's *his* fault, he thought, growing angry. She would have taken us to Puerto Rico. If it wasn't for *him! He* will never help Fernanda.

17

THE ACCIDENT

Reaching his own roof, Tomás walked more briskly. Fernanda would want to hear about the beach. She would expect him to be happy. If only he had the shells he'd collected. On impulse he stuck his hand in his pocket: sure enough, there were three. He took them out—one dark blue, one pink, one white shell—*and* a smooth white pebble.

He put them back in his pocket, pattered across the roof, and started down the iron ladder in his usual sure-footed fashion. But, somehow, he stumbled. He lost his grip on the side of the ladder, fell and hit the landing, his weight all on one foot. As he crashed against the barred railing, his ankle turned.

Pain shot up his leg. He ground his teeth to keep from screaming. Tears sprang to his eyes.

Fernanda shrieked and came running to the window. "Tomás! *Qué pasa?* Ay! *Madre de Dios!*"

He rocked back and forth, gasping, unable to speak or think.

Fernanda tried to haul him inside, but he shook her off.

"Are you badly hurt?" she kept demanding.

"I don't know."

Slowly, slowly the pain eased. He dared not move his foot for fear the hurt would begin again. He wiped his eyes and his sweating face on his sleeve.

Gently he eased himself on his hands to the window and swung his legs through. Gingerly, he put his weight on the other leg and stood up. With Fernanda's help, with ouches and *ays,* he reached a chair.

Fernanda untied his shoe and propped his leg on a box. She had been drinking coffee. Quickly she mixed him a cupful.

Drinking it, he began to feel better. He reached in his pocket for the shells. They were unbroken.

"Look," he said, "aren't they pretty?"

By emptying his pocket he was also able to show her a handful of sand. "See, this is what the beach is made of. You can run in it and dig in it—and even pour it back into the water."

Now he looked at his ankle again. It was swelling. He was frightened. They soaked it in hot water, but it had no feeling, except of water burning his skin.

Against his will, Fernanda turned his foot this way and that until one unfortunate movement made him shriek and kick at her with his good foot.

"I'm sorry," she apologized. "I think it's broken."

152

"How can it be broken?" he scoffed. He believed that broken legs looked like broken tree limbs—bent and hanging.

"It will be all right tomorrow," he promised. "You'll see."

They ate supper and then Fernanda read from a book, asking Tomás to tell her the words she did not know. He fell asleep. Presently she woke him and helped him into bed.

In the middle of the night, his leg began to throb. Tomás moaned and rolled over. His foot and ankle continued to ache.

"Fernanda," he called. "Fernanda, my foot hurts."

He heard her moving, and felt her hands as she knelt beside him. "Could I have a drink of water?" he asked.

She brought him a glass of water and went back to bed, leaving him to doze and wake, and cry quietly to himself.

When he opened his eyes, the light in the room told him the sun was shining. Fernanda came in with coffee and bananas.

When he had eaten his breakfast, he limped out to sit in the kitchen. He watched Fernanda wash the dishes, then wash the clothes and hang them on a rope.

He wondered if Barbara would miss him. She had asked him to come that day for more posing. He had kept from thinking about her words, but now he heard the doctor's voice again: *Children are bad enough when they're your own, but somebody else's.* And her reply: *I suppose you're right. You always are.*

The pain in his chest seemed worse than the pain in his ankle.

When he made himself stop thinking of Barbara, he worried that Mrs. Salvador or Mrs. Pérez might send to Mrs. Malloy's building for him to baby-sit.

It did not occur to him that Barbara would be the one to hunt for him.

However, as that day passed and the next, Barbara grew worried. By the afternoon of the third day, she

154

was saying to Omar, "I hope he didn't get sick from too much sun." She decided to go and find out.

In the downstairs hall of the tenement, she read the mailbox names. Lorca. No box bore that name, but of course his aunt's name might be Salvador or Pérez.

Mrs. Pérez opened the door of 5A. Young Fidel peered around her skirts.

"Good morning," Barbara said. "Is this where Tomás lives? I haven't seen him lately. I wondered if he was ill."

"No-o, he not live here," began Mrs. Pérez. "He live up the street. There is another apartment there."

"Up the street?" Barbara echoed.

"Sí. Two block. Up the street. This way." She pointed north.

Barbara frowned. "I thought he lived here with his aunt."

"No. Not here."

"Oh," Barbara said, puzzled. "Thank you very much."

"I not see him either, for two, three day, maybe. He baby-sit for you, too, eh?"

"No, I draw pictures of children, and sometimes he poses for me." Barbara thanked Mrs. Pérez and went back down the worn staircase.

She started north along Greenwich Street, wondering what apartment house Mrs. Pérez was talking about. Something was odd. She was very puzzled. If Tomás doesn't live in that building, how did he get locked out on the roof? she asked herself. Maybe, she thought, his aunt does not have a Spanish name, and he *does* live in the building.

Just then, however, she saw the curtained windows of Mrs. Malloy's building. This had to be the one Mrs. Pérez meant. It was the only apartment house in the block. She stepped into the hall. A small sign said SUPER, APT. 5.

She reached Number 5's door and knocked.

"Who is it?" a voice inside shouted.

Barbara raised her voice. "I'm looking for Tomás Lorca."

The door opened. Mrs. Malloy was wearing a large black-and-white apron over her dress, and holding a broom. Orange Clancy rubbed against the broom, purring.

"And what would you be wanting with him, Miss?" she demanded.

"I took him to the beach Tuesday," Barbara began. "I haven't seen him since, and I wondered if he was sick."

"Come in, come in!" Mrs. Malloy swept Clancy aside with the broom and stood at attention like a sentry. Barbara stepped into the shining kitchen.

"Have a chair, have a chair," Mrs. Malloy ordered. "Do you live in Brooklyn?"

"No. No, I live down the street," Barbara said, again puzzled.

156

Mrs. Malloy's blue eyes grew round. "You've seen Tomás around here?"

"Yes." Barbara nodded. "Doesn't he live here?"

"That he does not." Mrs. Malloy shoved the broom in the corner and sat down. "If that don't beat Pat! The little devil told me they was going to Brooklyn to visit their godmother, and off they went—clothes and all. That was weeks ago."

"He's visiting an aunt," Barbara explained. "Doesn't he have an aunt in this building?"

Mrs. Malloy shook her head. "Not him!"

Barbara raised her eyebrows. "I've seen him every day or so till this week. First he said he was visiting his aunt at the apartment building next to the butter-and-egg place. Later he said he lived with his aunt. The Puerto Rican woman in that building said he lives here. She sees him every day or so, too," Barbara added. "I believe he baby-sits for her."

"If that don't beat Pat!" Mrs. Malloy repeated.

"You mean he doesn't have an aunt at all?" Barbara asked.

"No! Maybe he ain't even got a godmother. Let me see now—" She got up and began rummaging through a drawer in the white cabinet spotted with red roses. "Where did I put that name and address? Got it here somewhere. Saw it the other day."

"I gather Tomás's father only comes home now and then," Barbara said.

"Not no more, he don't." Mrs. Malloy paused in her rummaging. "That poor man's gone from this world, if you ask me—may his soul rest in peace. I can feel it right here." She clutched her stomach. "Malloy says he's gone to Puerto Rico. But I tell him he's wrong. Mr. Lorca wouldn't've just up and left those children."

"But if something had happened to him, wouldn't someone have let you know?"

"Who?" Mrs. Malloy asked.

"The police—"

Mrs. Malloy gave an immense shrug.

"The question is," Barbara insisted, *"where is Tomás?* Could he be staying with some other family around here?"

Mrs. Malloy turned her head slowly left and then slowly right. "There used to be a Puerto Rican family around the corner, but they moved months ago. . . ."

Whenever Mrs. Malloy was upset, she put on the teakettle. She did it now. When it began its shrill whistle, she asked: "Would you like a nice hot cup of tea or coffee, maybe?"

Barbara said she would. She was getting a tight, frightened feeling. She told herself not to be silly. Of course *someone* knew where Tomás lived. Eleven-year-old boys did not live by themselves. *Someone* was looking after him.

But who?

18

WHERE THERE'S SMOKE

Barbara sipped coffee while Mrs. Malloy found the godmother's name, got the phone number from information, and dialed. The Mrs. Fernanda Ravello who answered had, of course, never heard of Tomás.

Barbara and Mrs. Malloy now began to be really worried. Mrs. Malloy said over and over again that Mr. Malloy was due home in a little while and that when he came, *he* would know what to do. Her faith made Barbara feel more cheerful.

Soon they heard Mr. Malloy's step in the hall, firm and confident. The door opened, and in he came, round and curly as ever. He looked hot and sweaty. His thick gray hair lay in damp ringlets around his forehead. Even his eyelashes curled.

"This is Miss Ransome," Mrs. Malloy said. "She lives down the street."

Mr. Malloy said, "Pleased to meet you," and shook hands.

"What a day!" he went on, dropping his cap and lunch pail on the nearest chair. "Anything cold?"

"Wait till you hear this!" Mrs. Malloy said, opening a can of soda and pouring it over a glass of ice cubes. Mr. Malloy drank it while they told him about Tomás.

"So the kid never went to Brooklyn, after all," he said. "So he's living around here somewhere. Gotta be!"

"But Fernanda," Mrs. Malloy cried. "What about Fernanda?"

"She's with him, of course. As sure as my name's Patrick A. Malloy."

"And what are they doing for food?" Mrs. Malloy demanded. "How could he take care of her? How can they be keeping clean? Lord love us, Malloy, and here all this time I've been thinkin' they was safe in Brooklyn!"

"Take it easy," Malloy said. "That kid's no dope. He'd get along. He found you—" He nodded at Barbara. "You said you paid him for taking his picture, didn't you? Selling fish from the fish market, running an errand or two."

"And baby-sittin'," Mrs. Malloy put in. "He told Miss Ransome he did baby-sittin'."

Malloy nodded again. "Maybe he took their clothes to the launderette once in a while. Between them they hardly own more than a good handful."

"But where is he now?" Barbara's fear grew. "Last time I saw him he asked me to take him to Puerto Rico with me if I went this winter. And he wanted me to find

160

out about helping his sister."

Malloy leaned both elbows on the table. "You thought he lived next door because he came by the roof, eh?"

He shook his head admiringly and clucked. "I'll tell you where he's hanging out—imp that he is. It's as plain as the nose on your face. He's hanging out in one of those empty buildings up this block or another. There's dozens of places where kids like them could sleep and never be noticed. Never be noticed at all. Leave it to Tomás! He's been looking after himself since he was three and done a good job of it. And he's smart in school. I've seen his report cards."

Mrs. Malloy's face beamed. "Now didn't I tell you himself would come up with the answer? He knows this neighborhood, Lord love him!"

"Lived here all my life," Malloy bragged. "Used to be all nice houses here—"

"But what if he's sick?" Barbara interrupted him.

Malloy thought that over. "That kid's never been sick a day in his life," he announced, "but I'll take a look around."

"You can come with me," he added graciously, "if rats don't scare you."

They scared her, but they would not stop her.

"Now don't you worry," Malloy told his wife. "We'll find them. Want I should bring the girl back here?"

"Of course bring her back here. Where else would you take her?"

He turned to Barbara. "Maybe you'll want to keep the boy till we decide what's to be done."

"Oh, yes," she said.

Meanwhile, Fernanda worried. Three days had gone by, and Tomás's ankle was now blue and swollen. Only a little food was left.

If I dared to cross the roof, she thought, I could go to Miss Barbara for help. Perhaps after dark I could . . .

She had an idea. Tomás had told her that Miss Barbara sometimes painted on the roof. If I build a fire, while it is still daylight, she thought—a small fire that would make a little smoke—Miss Barbara might see it and come.

She put a crumpled newspaper into the fireplace and lit it. She glanced at Tomás in the next room. He had not stirred.

The paper burned too fast to give off much smoke. She lit another and another. Suddenly smoke billowed into the room, making her cough.

Tomás awoke. "What are you doing?" he screeched. He jumped up, forgetting his ankle, and sank back with a groan. "Put that out!" he shouted. "Get some water!"

Fernanda hated to be shouted at. She stalked out and came back with a bucketful. She hoped Miss Barbara had seen the smoke by now. Angrily she splashed water into the fireplace.

Tomás lay back. "I'll be all right tomorrow," he

promised. But he was still in pain and no better than he had been yesterday or the day before.

As Barbara and Mr. Malloy started up the street they heard fire sirens. They paid no attention: engines went clanging past every day or so. By the time they had climbed to the roof of the apartment house where the Pérezes, the Salvadors and Bert lived, the shrieking trucks seemed to have come to a stop down below.

"Better see what's going on," Malloy said, and led the way to the parapet at the front of the roof. By standing on tiptoe, Barbara could lean far enough over it to look down. Two red and chrome trucks were drawn up in front of the building, engines running, red lights flashing. A third was screaming down the street to join them. Men in black helmets and black rubber coats swarmed in every direction, opening fire plugs, connecting hoses. Several who were carrying axes walked methodically across the sidewalk and into the building.

"They're coming in here," Malloy said, astonished. "There's no fire in this building. Guess we'd better wait a minute to see what's up."

Sure enough, they heard trampling on the stairs, and then a booted, black-coated fireman burst onto the roof. He took a quick look around and turned back to shout down the staircase. "Tell that woman to stay inside. The fire's not in her building."

Another fireman came up the stairs, breathing hard, and another and another.

"Where's the fire?" the first demanded, seeing Barbara and Malloy. He shoved his helmet back to wipe sweat from his forehead.

Malloy shook his head.

"You folks see any smoke?" demanded the second.

"Not a wisp," Malloy said.

At that moment the fireplace in the cave room chose to send up one last puff. The little cloud waved above the chimney like a flag.

"There!" A fireman pointed. He set off at a run, his rubber boots thumping across the tarred roof. The others followed.

"Smoke from a fireplace? That's a fire?" Malloy shouted.

"It's an empty building," one of the firemen shouted back at him as they bounded across the rooftops.

"That'll be Tomás," Mr. Malloy said to Barbara. "Come along."

"Should we?" Barbara held back, afraid of getting in the firemen's way.

Footsteps sounded on the stairs. A hand slapped the metal door and flung it open. Barbara took a deep breath and ran after Mr. Malloy.

Three of the firemen disappeared down Tomás's fire escape; a fourth ran to the front wall and waved his arms at the men still down in the street below.

Barbara followed Mr. Malloy down the ladder and

in through the apartment window. He gave her a hand as she jumped from sill to floor.

The firemen were running in and out of doors.

"Someone's living here," one man shouted, noticing how clean everything was and the drying clothes.

Malloy looked at Barbara. "What'd I tell you?"

Before she could answer, a fireman shouted, "You folks live here?"

"No," they both shouted back.

One of the firemen came stomping up the dark stairs. "I been clear through," he announced. "You men get to that room up front? That's where the fire is. No place else."

"The door's locked," they yelled.

"Break it down," he yelled back.

Barbara stood half-hidden behind Mr. Malloy's broad back in the hallway and hoped no rats would be frightened out of the building. More and more boots came climbing down the fire-escape ladder outside the window.

Suddenly the light from a powerful flashlight filled the room.

"Stand back and give him room to swing," the fire chief ordered.

The ax glinted in the light, and the wood of the door splintered. At the second blow, the door burst open.

"Anybody in there?" A beam of light cut the darkness.

"Kids!"

"Two kids!"

"Hey, what is this? What're you kids doing here?"

At that moment, for one instant as the light hit them, Barbara saw two pairs of enormous black eyes in two small, pale faces—Tomás and Fernanda, huddled under a blanket.

166

A fireman pushed past Barbara with an air of authority.

She saw by his white helmet that he was the chief. The Market watchman was behind him, and behind the watchman was a policeman whose broad shoulders further blocked Barbara's view of Tomás and Fernanda.

"You turn in the alarm?" the chief was asking.

"I did," the watchman said.

The chief reached the room. "These kids start the fire? Okay. Get 'em out of here."

"That's him!" the watchman cried. "I knew when I saw the smoke." He rushed at Tomás and hauled him roughly to his feet. Tomás screamed as pain shot through his ankle.

With a roar Malloy plunged forward like a football tackle.

"Keep your hands off those kids!" he yelled.

"Bit me!" the watchman yelled back. "He bit me!"

The men all began shouting at once. No one seemed to see Tomás who was rocking back and forth on the floor moaning, "My foot, my foot!"

Fernanda's shrill voice cut through the din, "Eeee-yiii . . ." she yelled. "His ankle. It is broken, you pigs and dogs! If you hurt him, I will kill you all!"

Barbara hoped no one else understood Spanish.

There was a dead silence for a few seconds and when the men stopped milling around, Barbara saw that Mr.

167

Malloy was carrying Tomás into the daylight of the kitchen. Fernanda ran along at his elbow.

"I can say in my report that you'll take care of this?" the chief was asking the police officer as the last pair of firemen's boots disappeared up the ladder.

"Yes, sir," the officer said, swinging his night stick nervously.

The chief nodded and went out the window and up the fire escape.

Malloy sat on one of the two chairs and held Tomás on his lap. Fernanda stood at his shoulder.

The watchman looked at his bitten hand and was starting to tell the policeman for the third time how he'd suspected Tomás, when the policeman interrupted him and said, "All right, Ernie, go put something on that hand. I'll let you know if I need you."

The policeman turned his back on the watchman and bent to look at Tomás's swollen ankle. Tomás let the policeman move his foot this way and that.

"There might be a small bone broke," the policeman said.

"Que dice?" Fernanda demanded sharply.

Tomás told her in Spanish.

"Now—" The officer looked from Mr. Malloy to Barbara. "What is all this? Do these kids belong to you?"

Barbara began to explain, and the officer wrote some words in his notebook. He took Barbara's name and address and telephone number. Then he took Mr. Malloy's name and address and telephone number. "They'll have to go to the station for now. Welfare will take over on Monday."

Fernanda shrank behind Mr. Malloy's broad back.

"This child needs a doctor," Barbara cried.

The policeman sighed. "Lady, we have doctors."

"But the girl needs a psychiatrist." Barbara did not give up. "She never goes outdoors. She'll be terrified."

"How you going to get her out?" Mr. Malloy demanded. "You try to haul her up that ladder against her will, you're liable to hurt her."

Barbara explained about Fernanda. "My brother's a psychiatrist. He could treat her," she said finally.

The policeman looked at his wristwatch. "What do you want me to do? I can't leave them here. You want to take them home and give them a bath and be responsible for them until Monday, it's all right with me. But I gotta get them out of here."

Barbara and Mr. Malloy were quick to accept the responsibility.

"Okay," the policeman said, "I'll go call an ambulance. One of you can go along to the hospital with the boy. I'll have the doctor give the girl a shot to keep her calm. She won't be any problem at all."

Tomás was glad to hear Barbara say that she would go with him to the hospital and that afterwards she would take him home to her apartment. Fernanda would be taken straight to the Malloys, and when she woke up, she would find herself in familiar surroundings.

Tomás raised his chin and looked Barbara bravely in the eye. "Are you going to give us to Welfare?"

Barbara looked at Mr. Malloy. "I hope we can work out some other arrangement. Something they'd like better."

"We'll see," Malloy said, and Tomás had to be satisfied with that. It was Barbara and Mr. Malloy's turn to ask a few questions. They began by asking how he had hurt his ankle.

It seemed no time at all before there were footsteps on the roof again, and the policeman came back down the ladder with the doctor who was carrying a black bag.

The doctor jumped through the window, set his bag on the table, and opened it.

"This the girl?"

"Yes." The policeman put one arm around Fernanda's shoulder. Miraculously, she did not fuss. "Come over here by the window, honey," the policeman said. "The doctor wants to see your arm."

"What's that?" Tomás gasped, catching sight of a shiny glass tube and the point of a needle. The doctor held it up to the light.

Mr. Malloy's big hand closed over Tomás's mouth. "Shhh," Malloy said in his ear. "He won't hurt her."

170

The doctor dabbed Fernanda's arm with a piece of cotton. With a flick of his wrist he slid the bright needle under her skin before she knew what was happening or had time to see what he held.

Tomás saw her jump, but she made no sound. The next instant the needle was out, the arm swabbed again with the cotton, and the doctor was walking back to his bag.

"There. That didn't hurt, did it?" the policeman asked, letting go of Fernanda who flung herself across the room toward Tomás and Mr. Malloy, but Barbara caught her and held her close.

"Cálmate, cálmate," she said soothingly. "You're all right now. Pretty soon you're going to feel sleepy, and then we'll take you home to Mrs. Malloy."

19

A VISIT FROM WELFARE

Tomás was not allowed to stay until Fernanda grew sleepy. The doctor looked at Tomás's ankle, nodded, and said, "The ambulance is waiting. Let's go."

Malloy handed Tomás out the fire escape to the policeman, and with no trouble at all the policeman carried him up the ladder, across the roofs, and down the stairs. Tomás wished Bert, Mrs. Pérez or Mrs. Salvador could see him being carried off by a big policeman, but they met no one.

Barbara followed and climbed into the back of the ambulance to sit on a little seat near him. The policeman went back to Mr. Malloy and Fernanda.

The doctor came into the ambulance and sat beside the driver. They set off quietly.

"Isn't he going to blow the siren?" Tomás asked.

"I guess not," Barbara said. "You're not an emergency case."

But the siren did growl as they crossed Broadway. It didn't rise to its full shriek, but it did growl loud enough to stop traffic.

"Here we are," Barbara said.

At the hospital the driver lifted Tomás out of the ambulance and sat him in a wheelchair.

Tomás didn't know whether to be scared or whether to enjoy the ride down the corridor and into the examining room. Barbara was beside him all the way. After a while they wheeled him to the X-ray room where, Barbara explained, they were going to take pictures of the bones in his ankle.

While the X-rays were being developed and studied, a nurse wheeled him back to the examining room. There they sat and waited for a very long time.

"Do you think Fernanda is asleep by now?" Tomás asked, nearly asleep himself.

"I'm sure she is. I expect Mrs. Malloy has her all tucked in bed."

Barbara went out for a few minutes and came back with hamburgers. At last the doctor came. He reported that Tomás had no broken bones, but he did have a bad sprain. He took a big roll of bandage and wrapped it around and around Tomás's ankle and foot.

Tomás and Barbara went home by taxi, which was almost as exciting as the ambulance. The taxi man drove faster.

Barbara paid the driver to carry Tomás upstairs. When they opened the door, Omar barked crazily, as though to ask, "Where have you been all this time?" Owa the Siamese jumped down from the window sill and came to sniff Tomás's bare toes which were sticking out of the bandage.

"We'll unwrap the bandage so you can take a bath and soak your ankle before bed," Barbara told him.

She filled the big white bathtub nearly to the top with water and after he had bathed himself and put on his shorts to sleep in, she re-wrapped the bandage. Then she put him in her bed and said she would sleep on one of the pink couches.

"Tomorrow we must get you a pair of pajamas so you can be a proper invalid," she said. "Now, how about some hot chocolate?"

She went into the kitchen and he heard her whistling while she fixed the hot chocolate for them both. Then she read to him until he fell asleep.

On Saturday morning Barbara telephoned her brother. Barbara told Tomás to call him Doctor Charles. He came in the afternoon, bringing red pajamas for Tomás.

Tomás scowled, but the red pajamas and Doctor Charles's friendly manners made it hard to stay mad at him. Girls being what they were, Tomás thought Fernanda would probably like the doctor a lot.

Doctor Charles asked Tomás how he felt, and then said, "Tell me a little about your sister. Do you know why she doesn't like to go outdoors?"

"Maybe because of my grandmama," Tomás began. And he told the doctor about their life until now.

175

The doctor asked a question once or twice, and finally he said he would go talk to Fernanda at the Malloys'.

"Is there any message you'd like to send her?" he asked. The question reminded Tomás of Sabertooth and McCall.

"The cats! Our things!" he said, thinking how Fernanda would be worrying about her scrapbooks.

"Your things will be all right for a couple of days," Barbara assured him. "And I'll take a can of cat food to McCall and Sabertooth in a few minutes. I'll also make sure they have water."

"Could Doctor Charles take Fernanda her scrapbooks?" Tomás asked. "And maybe an old magazine? She would probably be more friendly if you took them to her."

"I don't see why not," Doctor Charles said, smiling. "That's a good idea. I couldn't have thought of so good an introduction."

Barbara looked through a stack of magazines lying on the coffee table and handed three to her brother. A fourth she gave to Tomás in case he got tired of reading and wanted just to look at pictures.

Barbara and Doctor Charles left by the roof door. Tomás found it hard to concentrate on either the book or the magazine while Barbara was away. He coaxed Owa over to the bed and patted him as he listened for Barbara's footsteps.

When at last she came, she called out, "Everything's fine. The cats were curled up asleep, waiting for you, as though nothing had happened. We found the scrapbooks and your clothes. Charles took Fernanda's to her along with the scrapbooks, and I've got yours."

Tomás was relieved. They talked and Tomás told Barbara how he got food every day and how Fernanda had made a comfortable home for them. Then he lay back on the pillows and feel asleep. He was very tired.

When he woke up, he heard the doctor talking to

Barbara in low tones in the living room. He wished he knew what they were saying, especially about Fernanda and Welfare.

The rest of that day and all of Sunday, Barbara fixed Tomás's meals on a tray, gave him books to read, and fussed over him like a baby, but he did not enjoy it. He couldn't wait to be outside again.

Finally Barbara said, "Why don't you talk to Fernanda for a while? Here, I'll dial for you."

"Let me," Tomás begged, so she gave him Mrs. Malloy's number.

He heard it ring, and then Mrs. Malloy's voice on the other end. He began to giggle so much he could hardly talk.

"Lord love you, it's Tomás!" she cried at last. "Fernanda!" And then Fernanda's voice came shyly over the wire.

"Oh, Tomás," she said as she grew used to talking on a telephone, "Dr. Charles is so nice! In a few days he is going to take me to his hospital and help me not to be afraid. Then I will go in the street, and to school —everywhere!"

"I will walk over and see you before you go," Tomás promised. "Tomorrow, or the day after."

On Sunday evening, he got out of bed and limped around the room.

178

"Remember what they said at the hospital," Barbara warned him, " 'Stay off that foot for at least three days.' "

"I want to be able to walk when Welfare comes tomorrow," he explained.

"That won't be necessary," Barbara said. "I'm just going to have a talk with them. I'm pretty sure you'll be staying with me till your ankle gets well."

Tomás flopped back onto the bed. "Then I hope it *never* gets well."

Barbara smiled and smoothed her hair. "Yes, you do. How would you go to school?"

Tomás scowled at her. What did she know about Welfare? "You don't need to care whether I go to school or not." He turned his back to her. "You won't have to worry. You'll never see me or Fernanda again after Welfare gets us."

"Tomás!" Barbara dropped down to sit on the bed beside him. "Where'd you ever get that idea?"

He told her about Juan García, and what the kids at school said.

"That is just plain not true. And to show you how wrong they are, I'll tell *you* that Welfare is so interested in your being taken care of that they're willing to pay *money* for your food and clothing! Anyhow, you don't really know what became of Juan García's family. Maybe Welfare found them a nicer place to live—"

"This is a nice place to live," Tomás said.

"I know. But I mean out in the country—"

"Juan García liked it here."

"But maybe now he likes it better there. You just can't know. Besides, we're talking about you and Fernanda. What would you say to staying here with me while Fernanda goes to a hospital for a few months, until she learns not to be afraid out-of-doors?"

"Would I ever see her again?"

"Of course, Tomás! You could even visit her every week."

"Is this what Welfare is going to do?"

"In a way. My brother works as a doctor for the City part of the time, and he has talked to Welfare about Fernanda."

"And he'd cure her?"

"Yes. There is every reason to hope so, my brother says."

"And after that?" he asked. "Then can we both live with you?"

Barbara put her arm around him and hugged him tight. "I'm afraid not," she said gently.

"I know." Tomás was resigned. "You're going to Puerto Rico."

"Not only that, but Welfare thinks children need a father as well as a mother."

"Then why don't they find my father?"

"They're trying," Barbara said.

Tomás's heart felt suddenly lighter. "If Papa comes back, then we won't have to worry, will we?"

180

"You don't have to worry, anyway. The first thing is to get Fernanda well. After that, we'll take the next step." She rose and started toward the kitchen.

"Hey!" Tomás cried suddenly. "Hey, Barbara, would Welfare give me the money? If they would, I could buy another stove and fix that place all up with window-glass, and we could go back there and not bother anybody."

Barbara shook her head. "No, they wouldn't give it to you. It has to go to a grownup."

"They could give it to you—and you could give it to me."

Barbara laughed and shook her head again.

Tomás shrugged. Things went like that. He thought of the Malloys. "Would Welfare pay for Fernanda, too?"

"Yes, I think so."

"Then maybe the Malloys would take us both. Mr. Malloy is too old to have to worry about more mouths to feed." Tomás quoted Mrs. Malloy.

"There's still a question of where you'd sleep," Barbara said. "Welfare may not think the Malloys have enough room for you." She looked at her watch. "Okay, that's enough talk for tonight. Lie back now. I'll bring you a glass of milk."

Tomás awoke very early. He could tell how early it was by the gray light at the front windows. Omar lay stretched asleep at his feet. No sound came from Barbara and Owa up front.

He had been dreaming. What was it? A nice dream. He tried to remember. He had been back in their hideout, that was it, only it was all clean. The floors were still gray, bare boards, but the walls were white. He frowned, trying to remember. It was the hideout, but the rooms were different. In fact, it was like the apartments in Mrs. Malloy's building—like his old home, except reversed—at the *back* of the building. Like the empty apartment behind the Malloy's, that was it! Number Seven.

No one lived in Seven. Something had gone wrong with the plumbing years ago. From time to time when a pipe or fitting was needed elsewhere, Mr. Malloy took it from there. Mr. Malloy said the landlord did not want to spend the money to fix up the apartment.

Tomás sat bolt upright. The idea came bright as sunshine: If Welfare would pay the Malloys money for Fernanda's and his food and clothing, then he and Fernanda could each have a room in Apartment Seven! *And* their own living room so as not to bother Mr. Malloy when he came home tired and wanted to read the paper or watch TV.

He could see the whole thing clearly. Fernanda sitting at a table in the front room, a lamp shining on the book in front of her—not a scrapbook, but a schoolbook. He could even see the dress she was wearing, a plaid school dress. As though this were a doll's house with the roof cut away, he could see Mr. Malloy in front of the TV with his shoes off.

182

No, he was wrong. What he saw was himself and Fernanda, not studying but doing dishes in Mrs. Malloy's kitchen. Then Mrs. Malloy was plopping down in a chair near her husband. "Lord love those children!" she was saying. "They're as good as gold."

Maybe she wouldn't say just that, Tomás thought, coming back to reality, but she does like Fernanda, and I could run errands and do lots of things for her.

Impatient for Barbara to awake so he could tell her his idea, Tomás nudged Omar onto the floor with his good foot.

"Go get her," he whispered. But Omar yawned, stretched, and jumped back onto the foot of the bed.

He had to wait to tell Barbara until she was cooking breakfast.

"It sounds like a good plan," she said cautiously. "It's up to the Malloys, of course, but I can speak to them tonight—after we know what Welfare is going to say."

Welfare that morning turned out to be just one man wearing a brown suit. He introduced himself as Mr. Ross.

"Are you sure this is Welfare?" Tomás whispered to Barbara.

"Yes, I am. Why?"

"I thought they wore black uniforms with gold badges, and gold buttons, kind of like cops."

The talk with Mr. Ross took almost all morning. Barbara proposed to keep Tomás while Fernanda spent a month or two in Doctor Charles's care. By that time, she hoped Welfare would be able to find out what had happened to Papa. They told Mr. Ross the whole story, beginning with the time when Papa had not come home.

Then without warning Barbara said she was going to take Omar for a walk. Tomás was left alone with Welfare.

It was not so bad as he expected. In fact, it was not bad at all. Mr. Ross was nice. He just asked questions, like a teacher, and Tomás answered them all. Yes, he felt bad about Papa's being gone. He liked the idea of staying with Barbara. He did want to go back to school.

At last Barbara came in.

Mr. Ross said he was sure everything could be worked out as Barbara wanted it. He promised to come back in two days with papers to fill out.

20

REACH FOR THE MOON

One evening three months later, Tomás was again opening a door and stepping onto a roof. This time he had a right to be there: it was the roof of the Malloys' building.

In one hand he carried an old telescope that belonged to Mr. Malloy. He opened it up and steadied it against the chimney and trained it on the moon. He had to make a report on the moon at school tomorrow. But he had to hurry because Doctor Charles was bringing Fernanda at eight o'clock. That was when the party would start. It was all for Fernanda. At the Malloys. And Barbara was coming.

The morning after Tomás had told Barbara about his idea of living in Number Seven apartment, Barbara had talked it over with the Malloys.

"Bless my soul, did you ever see the like of him!" Mrs. Malloy had exclaimed. "Malloy, is there any reason under heaven why not!"

Tomás had watched Mr. Malloy, not breathing, just hoping.

Mr. Malloy was shaking his head, but there was a twinkle in his eye. He turned to Tomás. "When two women get their minds set," he said to him, "you might as well give in." He looked at his wife. "You got your heart set on raising 'em. Go ahead."

"Oh, boy!" Tomás ran to give Mrs. Malloy a quick hug, and she folded him in a hug so tight he had to wriggle free to breathe.

They talked about fixing the bathroom and painting the rooms, and Barbara offered to pay for it. Then she and Mrs. Malloy talked to Mr. Ross of Welfare and the landlord. A few days later Barbara reported to Tomás that the Malloys had been to the Welfare office and that Mr. Malloy had then gone uptown and talked to the landlord about breaking through the wall between the Malloys' apartment and Number Seven and making a door. The landlord was agreeable and set a very low rent for Apartment Seven. A week later Welfare advised the Malloys that the living arrangements had been approved.

That was more than three weeks ago now. What with school and helping get Number Seven painted and furnished, he had not had much time to visit Barbara. He was eager to tell her that Mr. Malloy said he worked better than the helper he had on the job.

And now Fernanda was coming home—home to the Malloys, to a real bedroom of her own, and a living room to be shared with Tomás. It was all just as he had dreamed it might be that morning months ago at Barbara's.

Tomás and Mr. Malloy had painted and painted and painted, until now the rooms looked brand new. Their belongings from the other place were stored in the kitchen, waiting for Fernanda to decide where to put them. And Mr. Malloy had brought their beds, the TV, and the other furniture up from the basement. With his help, Tomás hung George Washington and the map in the living room. Mr. Ross paid them another visit and thought everything looked fine.

Mrs. Malloy said it would not be necessary for Tomás to get free vegetables and fish from the markets any more, so he promised to help her in other ways.

Now, Tomás thought, gazing through the telescope at the craters on the moon, everything is going to be wonderful if Fernanda is really cured and if only she will like going to school! Then he remembered Papa.

He turned the telescope from the moon to a star. Mrs. Malloy said Papa was up there somewhere, higher than the trails of jet smoke, higher than the satellites and the moon. Papa had not stopped coming home because he stopped loving them. He had been killed in a traffic accident. The police had found a card in his pocket. It had his name on it, but no address. And after many weeks the police finally traced him to Mrs. Malloy's.

Tomás had cried when Barbara told him. He remembered how she had dropped into a chair beside the table and held him close, and he had cried and cried until her shoulder was all wet. Afterwards, as she wiped his face with a washcloth, he had bragged, gulping, "I never cry."

"Me neither," she had said, and he saw that her eyes were red, too. Without being told, he knew she must like him a lot if seeing him cry made her cry, too.

Tomás picked up the telescope. He closed the roof door behind him, locked it, and started downstairs. He heard voices and laughter below. Then Fernanda came running up the last flight of stairs. Barbara and Doctor Charles were with her.

"Tomasito," she called, catching sight of him. "I'm here! I'm home!"

She was wearing a pink and white dress that he had never seen before. A pink band was holding back her hair. She looked beautiful, and almost grown up.

"I came all the way here in Doctor Charles's car, and I wasn't afraid. Not the least bit," she was saying breathlessly. She hugged and kissed him until he pulled back through the apartment door.

She gasped to see the new white walls. Sabertooth came out of the bedroom, stretching and yawning.

"How big he is!" Fernanda cried.

"Look!" Tomás was calling. "Here's your desk, and your lamp, and over here—here's mine. And come in here—"

188

Doctor Charles and Barbara followed them from room to room, with Tomás proudly acting as guide. The Malloys brought up the rear. Everyone talked at once, shouting to make themselves heard. Then they all trooped into the Malloys' living room to have the ice cream and cake.

To make the occasion even more festive, there was a present for Barbara. Fernanda had finished the apron, and wrapped it neatly.

"It is for you," she said, laying it in Barbara's lap. It was beautiful. The ruffle was exactly right, and when Barbara put the apron on, the strings tied in a crisp bow. Tomás nearly burst with pride. All evening, too, he had been noticing how easily Fernanda spoke English.

At last Doctor Charles and Barbara rose to go.

"Omar will be wild with delight when he finds you're going to walk him every day," Barbara said, referring to the new job she had offered Tomás.

"Fernanda can come visit you, too, can't she?" he asked.

Doctor Charles smiled at her. "She certainly can."

Barbara and he said goodnight and went downstairs, and then Fernanda and Tomás said goodnight to the Malloys and went through the new door into their own living room. Sabertooth ran to them, and Tomás scooped him up and handed him to Fernanda.

"Isn't it nice?" Tomás said to Sabertooth who was

purring in Fernanda's arms. "When you lived with us before did you ever dream we would have such a place?"

Fernanda looked around the living room. "Oh, it's beautiful, Tomás, just beautiful!" she said.

"It was nice before, too," Tomás said, loyal to the hideout, "but I think everything is going to keep getting nicer all the time."

After Fernanda had gone to bed, Tomás settled himself at the table that held his new lamp and his schoolbooks. He picked up his composition. Now he knew how to end it.

"Once people said you were crazy if you reached for the moon," he wrote. "But some men did it anyway. If you do not try, you never get to the moon or anywhere."